Secrets of the Duke's Family

The mysteries and passions of the aristocracy!

Lady Margaret and Lady Olivia are hoping their brother, the Duke of Scofield, will sponsor a season for them. They're desperate to start their lives and to find the fairy-tale romance that awaits them in society's ballrooms.

But with rumors circulating that the duke murdered their father to get the title, scandal stalks the family wherever they turn. They must weather the storm as the truth is revealed...and as they fall, unexpectedly, irresistibly in love along the way!

Read Margaret's story in:
Lady Margaret's Mystery Gentleman

Read Olivia's story in:
Lady Olivia's Forbidden Protector

Read Rachel and Hugh's story in:
Lady Rachel's Dangerous Duke

Don't miss Christine Merrill's
Secrets of the Duke's Family trilogy

Available now!

Author Note

In this, the third book of the Secrets of the Duke's Family, we finally get to Hugh's story and his interaction with the Bow Street Runners.

The Runners were organized in 1749 and operated out of the Bow Street magistrate's office. They were formed by Judge Henry Fielding, whom some of you may know as the author of *Tom Jones* and one of the first English novelists.

Before that time, it was the responsibility of the public to respond to cries of "Stop, thief!" or "Murder!" and help with the apprehension of the criminal. That, along with the fact that the victims had to pay the costs of prosecution, made early policing pretty unreliable.

By 1815, when my story takes place, the Runners were already past their heyday and would merge with the Metropolitan Police in 1829.

CHRISTINE MERRILL

—

Lady Rachel's Dangerous Duke

Recycling programs for this product may not exist in your area.

ISBN-13: 978-1-335-40786-3

Lady Rachel's Dangerous Duke

Copyright © 2022 by Christine Merrill

For questions and comments about the quality of this book, please contact us at CustomerService@Harlequin.com.

Harlequin Enterprises ULC
22 Adelaide St. West, 41st Floor
Toronto, Ontario M5H 4E3, Canada
www.Harlequin.com

Printed in U.S.A.

Christine Merrill lives on a farm in Wisconsin with her husband, two sons and too many pets—all of whom would like her to get off the computer so they can check their email. She has worked by turns in theater costuming and as a librarian. Writing historical romance combines her love of good stories and fancy dress with her ability to stare out the window and make stuff up.

Books by Christine Merrill

Harlequin Historical

The Brooding Duke of Danforth
Snowbound Surrender
"Their Mistletoe Reunion"
Vows to Save Her Reputation

Secrets of the Duke's Family

Lady Margaret's Mystery Gentleman
Lady Olivia's Forbidden Protector
Lady Rachel's Dangerous Duke

Those Scandalous Stricklands

Regency Christmas Wishes
"Her Christmas Temptation"
A Kiss Away from Scandal
How Not to Marry an Earl

The Society of Wicked Gentlemen

A Convenient Bride for the Soldier

The de Bryun Sisters

The Truth About Lady Felkirk
A Ring from a Marquess

Visit the Author Profile page
at Harlequin.com for more titles.

To Havoc,
who was with me through more books
than I can count. Good boy.

Chapter One

'No.'

When it came to proposals, Rachel Graham had said the word a dozen times to a dozen different men and felt no desire to change her answer. It was not that there was anything wrong with Lord Perriman, who knelt before her, the perfect image of what a supplicating suitor should be. It was simply that she had no intention of marrying anyone, now or ever.

'You are practically on the shelf,' he reminded her, unconvinced by her refusal. He had lured her away from the Duke of Belston's ball to a remote sitting room to make this proposal in private. Now he was giving her a look that had nothing to do with the sort of love and devotion Rachel expected to see in a candidate for her hand. 'I do not think you have the time to be particular when it comes to marriage.'

'And I do not think a true gentleman would remind me of the fact,' she said, moving back on the settee to put distance between them.

'I have your father's permission,' he added, as if this would make a difference.

'You should marry him, if he is so fond of you,' she said, annoyed. After three years of her being in the marriage mart, her father was more than willing to give her to any man that asked. He did not understand that this casual attitude towards her future happiness made it even less likely that she would say yes to a man of his choosing.

Lord Perriman rose, brushing off the knees of his breeches as if he was shaking off her rejection. 'I doubt you will get a better offer.'

'I will take my chances,' she said, rising from the settee and walking towards the closed door. She stopped by it and pointed a finger at it as if she had the power to command him from a room that was not hers.

He gave her a speculative look. 'If we are found here unchaperoned you will have to marry me, you know.'

The thought was an alarming one. She liked the idea of a forced marriage to him even less than the politely arranged one he had been suggesting. 'We will not be found,' she said firmly.

'If there was a commotion, we might,' he said, still considering. 'If you should cry out, for example.' His arms were reaching for her as he stepped between her and the door.

'I have no intention of crying out,' she retorted, glancing round her for a weapon but finding none.

'Then you will be a willing participant in what happens next. That is, in my opinion, far better.'

'Or you could leave the poor girl alone. She has said no, and a true gentleman would accept her answer.' It was a voice that she had not heard in two years, yet it was as familiar as the beating of her heart. But Rachel doubted that Perriman was as well acquainted as she with the man who they had not noticed sitting in a darkened corner of the room. Thus, he did not share her desire to sink through the ground in mortification.

There was a flare of light as a candle was lit from the banked ashes in the fireplace. The Duke of Scofield stepped out of the shadows, his tall form even more menacing than usual in the half-light.

He had not been a duke when she'd known him, only Hugh Bethune. Nor had he been the talk of London, a man widely known as a cold-blooded killer.

'Really?' He directed the single word to Rachel in a tone of obvious disappointment. From his height of over six feet, he squinted down at her companion as if he were examining some lesser animal that had wandered into the house by mistake. 'Perriman, is it?'

The other man gave a moan of acknowledgement.

'You should make sure the room is empty before you start to make romantic overtures. And doubly sure if you mean to make threats.'

'I did not mean—' Perriman said hurriedly.

'How strange,' the Duke interrupted, his movements as slow as those of a cat stalking a mouse. 'You sounded quite sincere to me. Perhaps, if the lady wishes to leave us alone, we can discuss the importance of honesty—or, for that matter, honour—when speaking to the fairer sex.'

'That will not be necessary,' Rachel assured him hurriedly. Considering Hugh's reputation, she doubted that the unfortunate Lord Perriman wished to be anywhere near him, much less abandoned to face him alone. 'I believe my friend is aware of his mistake and wishes to go back to the ball.'

'That would be best,' Perriman said, grabbing for the door handle.

'Go, then. And if I hear that you have said a word about what happened here…' The Duke shrugged. 'That would be most unfortunate.'

'Of course, Your Grace,' Perriman said in a faint voice, then disappeared and left the two of them alone.

Rachel made to go after him. But before she could leave the Duke reached over her and leaned a hand against the door, shutting it. 'It is better that you wait here a few minutes and arrive back at the ballroom alone,' he reminded her. His voice had lost its menacing edge, but it was still different from the lover's tone she remembered.

It annoyed her.

But most of all it bothered her that, after all this time, her heart still beat faster at the sight of him.

Without meaning to, she was searching his face for differences from the man she had loved two years ago.

It seemed that, for him at least, far more time had passed. She thought she saw a few strands of silver shining amongst the gold, and his eyes no longer lit with mischief as he smiled at her. Instead, he looked tired and a little sad.

'The last time I spoke with you, you did not care for me or my future,' she reminded him. She had accosted him in the street to offer condolences on the death of his father. She had expected some sign that they would meet in private to discuss it. Instead, he had given her the same look he'd just used on Perriman and dismissed her as if they had no history at all.

Was it a flicker of the candlelight, or did she see him flinch at the memory? 'What I did in the past was for your own good.'

'For weeks you told me that you loved me,' she said. 'And then, when you should have needed me most, you pretended not to know me.' Of course, the words of love had been said in private. In public, it had been a different matter entirely.

'I did not think you would wish to be associated with a murderer,' he said with a bitter smile, and she saw the lines forming at the corners of his sea-green eyes, making him look much older than his twenty-nine years.

'We both know that the rumours are not true,' she snapped. 'I was with you in your room the night your father died, and I saw your face when you learned of his murder. You knew nothing about the crime. I'd have told the Bow Street Runners the truth if you'd asked me to.'

'And ruined your reputation in the process,' he said with a shake of his head. 'You should not have been in the house at all, much less alone with me.'

'We were doing nothing wrong,' she insisted. He had promised marriage and all the pleasures that came with it. She still dreamed of his passionate kisses, the feel of his hand sliding up her thigh and the whispers of what they would do together as soon as he could secure an advance on his portion of the estate. 'I would not have been ruined had you wed me as you promised.'

And now he said nothing, just as she feared he would. Despite what he had claimed during their clandestine meetings, it seemed it had never been his plan to marry her. Apparently, time had taught her nothing for here she was again, alone with him and hoping for something that would never be. 'What happens if I am caught here with you tonight?' she asked.

If she had hoped for some assurance that he would make things right this time, she was disappointed again. He reached for the door and shot the bolt. 'This will prevent any surprise interruptions.'

Her heart jumped and she took a deep breath to steady it again. She willed herself not to look at him, for she was afraid of what she might do now that he was close enough to touch. 'You have done more than enough to protect my reputation, Your Grace. Too much, in my opinion.' And yet, not the one thing she wished above all others. 'If you would be so kind as to unlock the door and check the passageway for people, I will be going now.'

'A moment longer,' he said, a wistful note creeping into the deep, silky voice. His hand circled her wrist, the gentlest of manacles preventing her exit as effectively as the lock. 'Two at most.'

'We have nothing more to say to each other,' she replied, but her own voice was hoarse, as if rejecting the lie.

'You know that is not true. I, at least, have something to say.'

'Then say it,' she snapped, wondering if there were words that would make any difference after all this time.

'It is only that I am sorry,' he said, his voice low and urgent. 'I never meant to hurt you. I never meant to leave you. But there was no other way.' Then he turned her wrist in his hand, unbuttoned her glove and pressed a kiss onto the bare flesh where her pulse was beating.

Before she could respond, he unlocked the door and pushed her out into the hallway, shutting the door behind her.

That had been a mistake.

Hugh walked across the room and sank back into

the chair that he'd occupied when he'd been interrupted by Rachel and her suitor, trying to regain control of his feelings. It had been over two years, but the
memories of the kisses they'd shared were never far
from his mind. The brief taste of her flesh just now
had been like opium, heady and addictive, bringing the old senses flooding back until he'd wanted
to fall to his knees and beg for her hand as Perriman had done.

She was every bit as lovely as he remembered. Her
long black hair was piled on top of her head in a tan-
gle of braids and curls. Her eyes were still the same
clear blue as a country sky in spring. And her body…

He closed his eyes, remembering how much he
had seen of what was hidden tonight beneath a de-
mure white gown. He would give a year of his life
for another glimpse of those breasts.

When he'd realised she was in attendance tonight,
he had come to this room to escape a meeting. He
rarely received invitations to public gatherings and
had grown good at accepting only those where there
would be no chance that he and Rachel might meet.

But tonight his instinct had played him false, and
fate had been cruel. He had been forced to sit mute
while another man had proposed to his beloved.
The relief when she'd refused marriage had been
as strong as it had been unreasonable. He had no
right to care about her future. She was free to marry
whom she liked.

He could not help but notice that in two seasons

she had not married anyone. And she had refused Perriman just now. It raised the unattainable dream that somehow they could still be together.

But he was not free. He had his sisters to think of, and the family's tainted blood. His father's murder, and the unspeakable things that had happened afterwards, had convinced him that the world would be better off if none of the Bethunes reproduced. Margaret had escaped him for marriage and a home of her own. Even if Olivia magically disappeared from his house and care, there was his own black reputation to consider before seeking a wife.

Title-hunting mothers might forgive a little drinking and whoring, and claim that reformed rakes made devoted husbands. But none of them were likely to tell their daughters that a murderer fell into the same category. Instead, they frightened the girls with cautionary tales of the Duke of Scofield and the fate of anyone who crossed him.

Only one woman knew the truth, or as much of it as he was able to tell. But just now she had given no indication that she wished to renew their acquaintance, even though she was free to do so. Perhaps it was time to stop torturing himself, dreaming of the one woman in London who he wanted but could never have.

Chapter Two

The next morning, Rachel sat with her parents at the breakfast table, her mind still on the meeting of the night before.

'Scofield was at the Belston ball last night. Can you believe the nerve of the man? Mixing with polite society as though he has any right to.' Her mother was buttering a muffin with short jerks of her knife, as if punishing it for the Duke's presumption.

'He is a peer,' Rachel's father pointed out in a reasonable voice. 'As such, he has the right to go almost anywhere. If Belston did not turn him out, there was little that the rest of us could do other than quietly disapprove. I expect we will see more of him before the season is through. They are scheming on some bill in the House of Lords, and it requires that Scofield at least appear to his equals to be a reasonable man.'

'They should snub him,' her mother suggested. 'He is, when all is said and done, a murderer.'

'Accused murderer,' her father replied. From his lower-ranked position of an earl there was little he could do about the behaviour of a duke other than to keep his opinions to himself. But when he was at home he spoke freely. 'Of course, in the two years since his father's stabbing, there has never been another suspect, nor was there any sign that the murderer came from anywhere other than inside the house.'

'It was right next door and we saw and heard nothing,' her mother recalled. 'The Bethune dog did not bark at all.'

In Rachel's too informed opinion, this meant very little. She had sneaked out of her own house and past Caesar the pug often enough to know that he could be bribed to silence with a soup bone.

'But still, he has not been convicted of a crime,' her father replied. 'A title goes a long way in protecting a man who made no bones about his dislike for the old duke. And, according to the servants, he threatened his father's life at the dinner table that very night.'

'Suppose he is innocent?' Rachel said, trying to drop the suggestion into the conversation without drawing attention to herself.

'Then he is a damned fool for not saying so. He should be shouting from the rooftops that he is unjustly accused. Instead, he seems to go out of his way to appear guilty. He makes a joke of his reputation and casually talks of ending the lives of those who cross him.' Her father shook his head. 'And then, there is the matter of Richard Sterling, who was found stabbed and dumped in the Thames after arguing with Scofield. Two murders in his past are more than a coincidence.'

'It shows a kind heart to think well of him, my dear,' her mother said, turning to her. 'But you do not know him as the rest of us do.'

'Of course not,' Rachel agreed, starring down into her chocolate and losing herself in memory.

She had been but a child the first time she had seen Hugh Bethune from her bedroom window, walking in the garden with his little sisters. And even then she had not been blind to what a handsome young man he was—tall and blond, with broad shoulders and the features of a prince in a fairy tale. She had thought that some day this was the sort of man she would want to marry.

She had not confessed the idea to her friends or his sisters, knowing that they'd have teased her unmercifully if they'd known the truth. Instead, she had kept her feelings for Hugh a cherished secret, dreaming of the day she might be old enough and pretty enough to catch his attention.

Years had passed before he had noticed her watching him from her window. Long enough for her fleeting thoughts to have developed into a full-scale infatuation. Once he had smiled and waved in her direction, and the greeting had been the only topic in her diary for weeks to come.

When she had finally grown old enough for a season, she had hoped above all else that he would notice her again. He had, only to explain politely that, though he might have liked to pursue her, he could not afford a wife. His father, Old Scofield, had been notoriously tight-fisted in money and affection, refusing his son a courtesy title and keeping his allowance to the bare minimum. Until the old man changed his mind—or, God forbid, died—there would have been no marriage for Hugh Bethune.

She had smiled and reminded him that it cost nothing to talk with a neighbour over the garden wall.

And so it had begun. Covert conversations from their respective gardens had led to a few all too brief dances at balls and long chats at routs.

And then she had suggested that she visit him in his room. He had argued that it was improper but had been impressed by her daring. And in no time his objections had given way to an invitation.

The house had been dark, for Hugh's father had skimped on candles as much as he did on any other household expense. It had made it easier for her to remain anonymous, the hood of her cloak pulled low over her face as she'd knocked on the kitchen door which had been opened by the housekeeper, bribed and sworn to secrecy by Hugh.

Without a word, she led Rachel to the servants' stairs, pointed up then turned away with the slightest sniff of disapproval.

Rachel had climbed alone and had been met at the top by Hugh, who'd wrapped her in his arms and escorted her to his room. And then, when the door was closed…

'Rachel!'

She started out of her reverie and looked at her father.

'Once you are done with your breakfast, I wish to see you in my study.'

'Of course,' she agreed, her mouth suddenly dry.

When they were alone a short time later, her father did not bother with preamble. 'Perriman says you refused him last night. In fact, you frightened him away. He was in a mad rush this morning to withdraw his offer.'

'He was not for me,' she said, purposely omitting the details that had soured him for her.

'The man had fifteen thousand a year and an excellent family,' her father snapped. 'And you refused him.'

'Because I did not love him,' she replied, praying that this would be enough of an explanation.

'Love,' her father said with a huff. 'That is a thing for the lower classes. You need to have more sense.'

'I am sure there is another man who would suit me better,' she said with an embarrassed shrug.

'Then name him and I will arrange a match,' he replied.

For a moment, Rachel considered telling him the

truth. But, judging by the conversation at breakfast, there was no way they considered Hugh as a suitable husband for her, so she held her tongue.

Her father noted her silence and shook his head in disappointment. 'I did not want to discuss this matter in front of your mother, because talk of what is to come only upsets her. But you, my dear, must understand that the estate is entailed to my cousin, and you and your mother will have very little when I die. Unless you are sensible and marry well.'

'Surely the situation is not that dire?' she asked. 'Your health is good.'

He laughed. 'You cannot see as far into the future as the tip of your nose. My health is fine, but I cannot afford to be short-sighted. None of us know our allotted span on this earth and our lives can change without warning. I want to see you settled, and soon, for your own good and that of your mother.'

'But not to Perriman,' she said, trying not to shudder as she thought of how eager he'd been to dishonour her to secure her hand.

'Then who?' he asked. 'Do you have someone in mind?'

'No,' she replied hurriedly, closing her hand over her wrist which still felt the heat of a kiss. 'I have met no one as of yet.'

'Then I suggest you take the next man I find for you. You talk of love, but that is a girlish fancy. Once you are married, you will find that security is even better than emotion, and not nearly as fleeting. The process of making a good match need not be as complicated as you are making it. I will find you a kind man who will make you a good and caring husband. In return, you will be a good wife to him.'

'I will try,' she said, unwilling to give him a definite yes without knowing the man he might choose. She had hoped that the final decision would be left to her and she might be allowed to keep her broken heart to herself and remain a spinster.

But that was before Hugh had kissed her.

Though it had hardly been a kiss, if she was honest. She had been courted by men who'd been far more forward than that. But none of their kisses had moved her as Hugh could with a single touch of his lips. It was clear that he still cared for her. But it seemed that, now that he had the money to do it, he was no more eager to marry than she was.

It was probably because most eligible girls were too frightened of the supposed murderer to allow him to court them. His dire reputation was unearned. She knew that better than any other person in England. If her family was worried about it, after the initial shock wore off, she was sure her father would be satisfied with a rich peer for a son-in-law.

The question was, how to make Hugh act on his attraction to her? It was rare to see him out in public, and last night was the first time in ages that she could remember having been at an event he'd attended. Even then, he had made no effort to imply that there would be anything more between them than that kiss of apology.

But he was wrong. She loved him then, she loved him still. If she had to marry, there would never be another man for her than Hugh Bethune.

'Hugh!'

The Duke of Scofield started, nearly dropping the brandy glass he had been holding. When it caught him unawares, the sound of his own name still cut through his heart like a knife slash, for it made him remember *her*.

He set the glass on the corner of his desk, wondering if Olivia would smell the liquor on his breath and question his drinking so early in the day. She had only herself to blame for that. In this, the second year of their mutual captivity, he was no closer to deciding what to do about her than he had been on the day that their father had died.

His younger sister, Margaret, had solved one problem for him by eloping. He was still not positive who had committed the murders, but he had not wanted it to be dear, sweet Margaret. Thus far, Peg's husband, the newspaper reporter who had stolen away with her, was annoyingly alive, as were all of their acquaintances.

If Peg had been the mad one, and she'd not been able to help herself from committing mayhem, then he should have seen some sign of it swirling about her now that she had ample freedom to act.

Olivia, however, had lost a suitor in the Thames. When it had happened, society had been quick to blame Hugh for the death of Richard Sterling. He knew his own mind and was sure of his innocence.

But Olivia's state of mind and innocence were other matters entirely. After their father's death, Hugh had done his best to contain both girls from leaving the house unescorted, fearing that the guilty one might attack again. But Olivia still got away from him on occasion. If he were a betting man, the money would be on her. She had always been the shrewder of the two girls, and the one over whom men were eager to sympathise about her evil brother and his cruel restrictions on her socialising.

She was calling him again but he ignored it and stood, stepped to the window and touched the glass, spreading his fingers until his palm was flat to the surface, reaching towards the house on the other side of the garden wall and the woman who was never out of his heart or mind.

Rachel had not yet married. He wished she would, for it would save him the torture of wondering if she still thought of him, and if any of those thoughts were kind. Last night, she had seemed more angry than pleased, for he was quite sure he'd broken her heart with the way he had treated her after his father's death.

She'd had every right to think he was going to make her a duchess. He had promised marriage often enough in those days, and the pledge of a future together had convinced her that it would not be too sinful to sneak next door and into his room for some early lessons in the art of love.

Perhaps it was the prolonged excitement and denial of climax, but no woman before or since had heated his blood in the way his sweet Rachel had. He had rushed to her that night, barely noticing one of his sisters darting down a darkened hallway and laughing as she entered their father's study. His mind had had room for nothing but Rachel.

They had been together for only a few minutes when the screaming had begun downstairs and the servants had come to summon him. His father was dead. Murdered.

He had rushed Rachel from the house moments before the Runners had arrived, away from the chaos that ensued. Then he had cut her on the street when she'd tried to reach out to help him. There was no help. Not for him and not for his sisters.

He had broken what was left of his own heart on that day, but it hardly mattered. His heart, his mind and his life were no longer his own.

'Hugh!'

He shook his head to clear it and answered, 'Here, Olivia.'

His sister stuck her head round the door of the study and stared at him, obviously annoyed. 'I have been calling for you all over the house and you did not answer.'

'Well, you have found me now,' he said in the

mildest tone he could manage. 'What do you wish of me?'

'The same thing I always wish of you. I would like to go to the same places you do without a phalanx of your hired guards escorting me.'

'You wish to go to Parliament or my club?' he said, being deliberately obtuse.

'You went to a ball last night,' she reminded him. 'At the Duke of Belston's townhouse. Why would you not take me along?'

'I would not have gone myself, except I need his support for a bill I am putting forth. If not for politics...' He shrugged. 'And last night you were too inebriated to leave the house.'

'It is unfair of you to remind me of that,' she said with a wince. 'I would not have drunk so much ratafia if...' She stopped, unwilling to admit the difficulty that had caused her to resort to consoling herself with spirits. The man he had hired to watch her had caught her attempting to elope with her current beau, Alister Clement. Clement had been left in a ditch on the road out of London and she had been brought home in disgrace.

'I admit I was indisposed last night,' she allowed. 'But I am fine now. Let me accept one of the other invitations you receive,' she said with a longing tone that might have influenced him had she been a normal girl. 'There is no need to keep me locked in this house, nor to have me watched.'

He could not help a bitter laugh. 'It would be easier to believe that if you had not helped Margaret to elope a few months ago.'

'I did not help her. She did what she did on her own. It had nothing to do with me.' He was sure it was a lie, for the denial came too quickly, as if it had been rehearsed.

'You did nothing to stop her,' he reminded her. And now, you wish to go about without even your ster for chaperone.' She was looking for an excuse meet with Clement. Hugh had forbidden the fellow om courting Olivia more than once, and yet he did t leave. Nor, it seemed, did he have the brains to an a successful elopement. After his last attempt, ivia had retreated to her room with a decanter of afia to sulk and drink herself silly.

It was fortunate for Clement that she had turned r anger inward instead of against him. He might ve ended up as dead as Sterling, the last poor sod t had not managed to spirit her away.

his morning, she was sober again, though as she led encouragingly at him she squinted at the sun- t as if it hurt her eyes. 'Peg may be gone, but you rust me.' Her voice was plaintive, but it did not the lie. He had lost the ability to trust either of sters on the day their father had died.

y rule stands,' he said. 'You will not go about unaccompanied by a servant and you have no to go to social gatherings in the evening while still in mourning.'

have been out of mourning for over a year,'

she snapped, gesturing to her gown, which was a light blue.

'But that does not mean that you need to rush back to socialising. If you need fresh air, you may go to Bond Street, as long as Mr Solomon is there to watch over you.'

'I would rather stay home than go anywhere with your watchdog,' she said with an unladylike grimace. For some reason, she had taken a particular dislike to her latest guard.

Perhaps it was because the fellow was doing his job. Yesterday had been Liv's and Clement's second run for Gretna, and Michael Solomon had stopped them both times.

'If you do not want to go out with the man I have hired to protect you, then stay home and stop complaining,' he said. His stand taken, he stared down at his desk, searching for a distraction to end the conversation. He grabbed a pile of papers and shuffled them, hoping that she would take the hint and leave.

'You cannot keep me here for ever,' she said.

'We will see about that,' he replied, and felt the door slam as she left his study. The thought of a lifetime trapped in this house with his sister was a nightmare. All the evidence pointed to the fact that she was both mad and dangerous. After what he had done to protect her from prosecution, maybe he was mad as well. But, if it kept her from the hangman noose, he would lock the doors against the world and they would stay here, together and alone.

Chapter Three

It was one thing for Rachel to decide that she would marry the most notorious man in London and another to get him to agree to it.

She brooded all night and most of the next morning, trying to think of a way to orchestrate another meeting with Hugh. Even though he lived next door to her, she had not seen him for two years before last night. It would take an astronomical amount of luck to run into him again in a day or two.

As a distraction, she took her maid and set off for Bond Street and a day of shopping. But not even a new bonnet was enough to take her mind off the problem.

At last, they settled for refreshments at Gunter's. Rachel stared down into a plate of delicate lemon biscuits, still unsatisfied. 'Tilly,' she said to her maid, 'What is one to do when one knows the man one wants to marry, but he is so reclusive that it is a trial to even meet him?'

The maid gave her a curious look. 'Is this a man that your parents would approve of?'

'He is purely hypothetical,' she said quickly, afraid to give away the truth, since she was sure that Hugh was exactly the opposite to what her father was hoping she would agree.

'Well, if Mr Hypothetical won't come to you, then you must go to him,' the maid said with a grin.

It was a simple answer. But perhaps this was a simple problem that she was making unnecessarily complicated. He was right next door. If she manufactured a reason to visit his sister, she might see him as well.

But there was a rumour about that Lady Olivia was still in mourning and not at home to visitors. The *ton* had given up attempting to gain entry. Surely that did not include neighbours? It had been years since Rachel had been close to Olivia, but that did not mean that she could not renew the childhood friendship they had shared. After all the time spent in seclusion, she would probably welcome anyone willing to see her. And, once the door was opened by the sister, the brother could not avoid her for ever.

Then, to her surprise, Lady Olivia walked into Gunter's escorted by a gentleman. But when Rachel looked closer she realised that he was not a gentleman at all. He was the man she had seen standing guard in the back garden of the Scofield townhouse. Hugh must have hired him to see to the security of the household.

Her new plan to befriend Olivia was abandoned as quickly as it had been hatched, for something about the posture of the two convinced Rachel that they had no desire for her company. Instead, she turned away from them and stared at their reflection in a mirror on the wall so she might study them without being observed. It was not that unusual to see a young lady escorted by a servant, but that was not how this looked at all. Liv seemed to be enjoying the man's company, chatting easily with him, smiling and leaning in to hang on his words as they gossiped over their food. As Rachel watched, Olivia leaned even closer, staring intently at the man who accompanied her.

This was an interesting development. She wondered if Hugh knew of it. More importantly, she wondered if he might want to hear of it. If it was true that Olivia was not allowed to mix with society and the gentlemen who might court her, it appeared that she had found a way round the restrictions. She was smiling at the man she was with, laughing at something he'd said. Her eyes sparkled as she looked at him. Then she tugged on a curl in a way that drew his attention to the shining gold of her hair.

He stared at it, and Rachel saw a flash of hunger in his eyes before he moderated his emotions and looked at her as a gentleman should, as if her words were more important to him then her looks.

Rachel's resolve wavered. It was spiteful of her to want to deny them their happiness. Perhaps she could make it up to them later. But for now, this sighting was something she could use to her own benefit. Tattling on his sister would give her an excuse to talk to Hugh again. But she had to get to him before he learned of it himself.

She emptied her teacup and told Tilly to gather their packages. Then, without acknowledging her neighbour, they summoned the carriage and returned home. When they arrived, Rachel announced that she was still in mood for a walk, and assured her maid that her company was not needed as she did not mean to go farther than down the street to stretch her legs.

Once out of sight of the girl, she hurried next door, knocked and requested an audience with the Duke.

As Hugh finished his third brandy of the day, a footman appeared in the doorway of the study and presented him with a calling card.

'Lady Rachel Graham?' he asked and felt the world tipping violently around him in a way that could not be blamed on the liquor.

'She insists that you will want to see her, once you hear what she has to say,' the footman replied, before Hugh could tell the servant to deny her entry.

'Show her to the green salon. I will be there shortly.'

The servant retreated and Hugh allowed himself a moment of panic, wishing that at least he had a mirror to see if he was presentable enough to receive visitors. Then he reminded himself that he was not required to dress for uninvited guests and, much as he wished to spend time with Rachel, he owed her nothing, nor was there anything she could do to help him. The sooner the visit was over, the better it would be for both of them.

He strode down the hall to the green salon and greeted her with a frosty, 'Lady Rachel?' trying to ignore how delightful she looked in a deep-blue walking dress.

'Since we are in private, is it necessary to be so formal?' she responded with a smile that made his loins ache.

'Since you are unchaperoned and uninvited, I would prefer formality,' he said, unsmiling.

'Well, the least you could do is sit down in my presence,' she said. 'You are making me nervous.'

Then they were both uncomfortable. He doubted sitting would make him feel any better, but he also doubted that it would make things much worse. He took a seat in the chair opposite to the settee she occupied and folded his arms. 'Very well. What brings you here today?'

'I am here because I have news that I think would interest you,' she said, then added, 'It is about your sister.'

'Which one?' he asked.

'Olivia,' she replied. 'I just saw her at Gunter's, having sorbet with a handsome man.'

His brow furrowed. 'Was he a gentleman with dark hair, sharp-featured with a slight build?' If Solomon had permitted a meeting with Alister Clement, Hugh would sack him without references.

'No,' she said with a sly smile. 'He was the man I sometimes see sitting in your back garden.'

'Solomon!' he exclaimed, relieved. 'The man is an employee and is doing his job as escort.'

'He did not look like an employee,' she said, sounding uncommonly smug. 'They looked quite cosy.'

'Really.' Apparently, the animosity Olivia had displayed towards him was all for show. She had taken it into her head to charm Solomon and the fellow, who had been on the job for less than a month, was already succumbing.

'And now, I suppose you are going to threaten to end him?' she enquired with a sigh.

If Solomon touched his sister, this time it would be more than a threat. 'If you did not want me to act, why did you bother to tell me?'

'I do not care if you act,' she said. 'But I hope you will spare me the false threats that you scatter about London like breadcrumbs for birds. I know you too well to believe them.'

He did not think that she would be fooled, but that did not mean he owed her the whole truth. 'I am not the man you remember,' he said, rubbing his temples to dissipate the headache gathering there.

'You are more,' she said without hesitation.

'I have a title,' he said. 'And the money, of course.'

'And I am sure you manage both with wisdom

and skill.' She was smiling at him, as if admiring an honour he had done nothing to earn.

'Next, you will be telling me that my father would be proud,' he said with a bark of laughter. 'We both know that he hated me and would have lived for ever, if he could have, just to deny me the succession.'

'But that does not mean you wanted him dead or were capable of doing what everyone thinks of you,' she returned. 'I ask you again, why do you make no effort to clear your name?'

He wanted to speak, but the words would not come. It would be such a relief to talk about what had happened after she had left him that night. But, other than a brief respite from the pain, it would change nothing. At last, he said, 'Because sometimes it is better for people to believe a lie than to know the truth.' Then, he stood and gestured towards the door. 'Thank you for the concern you have shown my family. And now, the footman will show you out.'

'Wait,' she said, ignoring the servant and holding her seat. 'When will I see you again?'

'You will not,' he replied. This renewed contact with her was almost more than he could stand. Each moment she sat here, he could feel his resolve weakening and the growing urge to live selfishly, do what he most wanted and let the devil take the rest of the world. 'These recent meetings were aberrations, and they will not continue.'

'After what I have told you today, you owe me at least a dance,' she said, smiling again.

He shook his head. 'Perhaps your feelings are not as strong as they once were, or perhaps you do not understand how difficult these encounters are for me. But, I can assure you, we cannot and will not be together now or in the future as anything more than casual acquaintances. What we once had is over. I suggest from now on you make an effort to avoid me as studiously as I have been avoiding you. Good day, Rachel.' Then, as she showed no sign of leaving, he exited the room and went back to his study, slamming the door behind him.

That had not gone at all to plan.

Rachel had probably been naïve to hope that he would be grateful enough to welcome her information. But she had been positively stupid to think that he would reward her by agreeing to see her again.

At the door to the receiving room, a footman shifted from foot to foot, probably trying to decide the best way to put her out.

She smiled at him, making a great show of composing herself in preparation for leaving, while struggling to find a way to salvage the situation. He had called these meetings painful. And he had said it with what sounded like disguised longing in his voice. Despite what he might say aloud, he wanted her still. He loved her still.

If love was not dead, then she could not abandon him, no matter what he might claim to want from her.

She rose and followed the footman down the hall,

pausing again as she passed a console table on which the morning's outgoing post was stacked. Casually, she brushed against the letters, knocking them to the floor.

The footman rushed to grab them, but she was faster, scooping them up with an apology and placing them back on the table where they had been.

But not before taking note of the directions on several of the notes. Her mother had a similar stack of responses to dinners and balls leaving the house that very morning. If she wanted to see Hugh again, she knew exactly where to look.

Chapter Four

Two nights later, Rachel prepared for a ball at the Earl of Canfeld's home, taking pains to hide the nervousness she felt at the thought of the evening ahead. After years of avoiding and being avoided by Hugh, it felt odd to stalk him in this way, and to dress in a way that she hoped would please him above all others.

She chose a gown of green silk that would stand out from the crowd of virginal white that made up the usual wardrobe of unmarried females. With it, she paired the same gloves that she had been wearing the night he had kissed her wrist. She wondered if he would remember them.

When they arrived, she did her best to separate herself from the ever-watchful eyes of her mother and looked around her nervously as her dance card began to fill without any sign of Hugh's arrival.

When he did appear, she was on the floor and unable to go to him without slighting her partner and walking away in the middle of a dance. Instead of focusing on the steps, she watched over her shoulder as Hugh worked his way through the receiving line, made nice to his hostess and prepared to leave the room again, probably for the card room and the company of gentlemen.

She could not let him escape so easily. They were almost at the bottom of the set. Once there, she excused herself from her partner, claiming fatigue, and rushed down the hall that led to both the ladies' retiring room and the card room. She caught Hugh before he could disappear behind the door, calling, 'Your Grace, a moment of your time.'

He turned back to her with a look so dark that, for a moment, she had no trouble believing his evil reputation. 'How may I help you, Rachel?'

'I was wondering if you planned to dance this evening.'

Now, he simply looked annoyed. There was also nothing in his face to reveal that he knew her in any but the most remote of ways.

'No.' He did not bother to embellish the word with a reason.

'I wonder if you might reconsider,' she said. 'There are many of us who must go un-partnered for the lack of interest of the gentlemen here tonight.'

He was about to say no again. She could see it in his eyes. So she reached to the wrist of her glove and gave a deliberate flick, opening the button that he had undone when they had been alone at the last ball.

Exposing a single inch of skin was surprisingly effective. His eyes were riveted to the spot. He wet his lips, as if he was eager to taste, totally undoing his previous frosty greeting.

For a few seconds at most they were alone in the hall, out of range of hearing of the other guests. But people were heading down the corridor towards them, so she pressed her advantage. 'If you say no, it will appear that you have cut me. It will cause far more attention to our relationship than a simple yes will do.'

The look he gave her now smouldered with anger. 'We have no relationship. Not any longer.'

It was a lie. She was sure of it. So she refused to move on, letting the other guests grow close enough to hear the silence stretching between them.

When the strangers were almost upon them, he surrendered. 'Perhaps one dance would not be so unusual.'

'Of course not,' she said, offering her dance card to him. He had not chosen a waltz, but a simple country dance that required a minimal amount of physical contact. It was not as romantic as she'd hoped, but it would have to do to start with. She smiled up at him, unable to disguise her feelings. 'That was not so hard, now, was it?'

'More difficult than you can imagine,' he said, turning back to the card room and away from her.

As she went back to the ballroom, her mother caught her at the doorway and touched her shoulder. 'Your father said that you and Lord Perriman did not suit.'

'Do not worry,' Rachel said quickly. 'I am sure there will be other offers.'

'I have counted the guests tonight and cannot find a single one that you have not already rejected,' her mother said with a shake of her head.

'Not a single one?' Rachel resisted the urge to smile and correct her.

'No one acceptable,' her mother allowed. 'There are several who are so near to spoken for that it is not worth bothering.'

'Every night does not have to be a husband hunt,' Rachel reminded her. 'Perhaps tonight I will have to content myself with refreshments and dancing.'

'You are far too easily contented,' her mother said with a huff.

'It is better than being difficult to please,' Rachel shot back, fanning herself vigorously. 'And now, if you will excuse me, Mother, the music is beginning and I must go and find my next partner. I have no intention of being rude, even if nothing is to come of it.' And, even better, she must be ready for the moment when something did.

When the time to dance arrived, Hugh was surprisingly nervous. It was nothing, he told himself. He was a grown man, not a schoolboy, and had partaken freely in pleasures of the flesh far greater than a turn around the floor with an innocent young lady.

But was she innocent? He had not taken her maid-enhead, but he had done far more than he should have with a woman who'd not been betrothed to him. They had been so sure that marriage was only weeks away that she had allowed him liberties and he had accepted eagerly.

And then, everything had changed.

He had not even expected to see her tonight, since he normally avoided the ballroom at such gatherings. But she had found him, and he had succumbed far too easily to her plans. And there had been a plan, he was sure. She had sought him out twice now, and there was no sign she would stop. He must find a way to put an end to this before she became convinced that she was making progress in reuniting with him.

He approached her at the beginning of the chosen dance and wordlessly bowed over her hand, trying not to look too closely at the broad expanse of flesh displayed above the bodice of her gown. Then the music began and they moved in silence. But he could feel the eyes of the crowd following their every move.

'People are staring,' he muttered as they passed in the patterns of the dance.

'I should think you would be used to it by now,' she replied. 'From what I understand, people often stare at you.'

'But they do not stare at you,' he reminded her. 'In dancing with me, you have made yourself notorious.'

She smiled, unperturbed. 'I think I should rather like being notorious. It sounds much more interest-ing than being a wallflower, which I very nearly am.'

'You would not have to be, if you just accepted one of the offers you have got,' he reminded her.

'Like Perriman?' she asked and made a face. 'You were quick enough to save me from him when you had the chance. If you wanted me married, you could simply have remained quiet.'

'That was different,' he insisted. 'He was attempting to take advantage.'

'As you would have, if you wanted a lady enough,' she pointed out, giving no quarter.

'We are not talking about me,' he said through clenched teeth. 'We are talking about you.'

'And my need to marry,' she said with a sigh. 'You remind me of my father.'

'That is not what any man wants to hear from a beautiful young lady,' he said, then snapped his mouth shut to prevent any more inanities from escaping.

She laughed. 'Your Grace, did you just flirt with me?'

He hadn't meant to. And yet, when he was with Rachel, it was hard to do anything else. 'Do not put too much into it,' he retorted gruffly. 'I am well known as incorrigible.'

'And now you are joking,' she said with a smile that lit up the room. 'Given time, who knows what you might be capable of?'

The statement shocked him back to earth, for that was exactly what he feared. When one had already done unspeakable things, what else might lie in the future?

'I am not going to allow another dance, if that is what you are thinking,' he replied in a firm tone to caution himself as well as her. 'Everyone here will tell you this one was a mistake.'

'And I will not listen to them,' she said, still smiling. 'There is no harm in dancing.'

'If that is all you expect,' he replied.

'What else could I possibly want?' She blinked innocently, calling attention to her sable lashes and bright eyes.

'More than I am willing to give,' he shot back with a warning shake of his head. 'Do not try this trick again or, so help me, I will leave you standing in the hallway like the wallflower you pretend to be.'

And then, to his relief, the dance was over before she could think of anything to say in response. She dropped a curtsy, as if nothing unusual had happened, but there was a brittleness to her smile. As she turned to walk to the edge of the dance floor, he noticed a tightness in her shoulders, as if she were recovering from a blow.

And, God help him, it was all he could do to keep from running after her with an apology. To be with her set him free, and freedom was weakness. These meetings could not keep happening or he would shatter like glass, blurting his secrets to Rachel and anyone else who would listen. If he did not want to see his sister in the madhouse, he must be strong and stay away from Rachel Graham.

'Rachel!' Her mother rushed to her side as soon as she was free of Hugh and whispered, 'Whatever did you think you were doing, accepting a dance from that man?'

'It was only a dance, Mother,' Rachel replied, experimenting with a defiant roll of her eyes. 'We are neighbours and have known each other for years. And he is a duke. I could not exactly refuse him.'

'You most certainly could,' her mother said, pulling Rachel by the arm towards the door. 'If you did not notice, he did not bother dancing with any of the other young ladies here, probably because they all had the sense to say no.'

'He didn't ask anyone else,' she argued. Of course, he hadn't asked her either. She had bullied him into it and made him angry. They had not parted well. But there had been a moment—during the middle of the dance—when he had been his old self.

'I have no idea what reason he would have for singling you out,' her mother said. 'But we must be sure it does not happen again. For now, we are going home before you cause any more trouble.'

As she was rushed from the room, she caught the eye of the dangerous Duke of Scofield, who gave her a look that could only be described as, *I told you so.*

Rachel spent the night puzzling over the best way to proceed. It was clear after her parents' reaction that she could not treat Hugh as she would any other gentleman, dancing and flirting in the open. She did not mind the staring so much as her parents' response to it. She would never have a chance to weaken Hugh's resolve if she was rushed out of the room and home each time they danced together.

Nor did she think Hugh would come if she invited him to meet in private. He was far too conscious of his reputation and hers. But at the Belston ball he had jumped to her defence the minute he'd thought she was in danger.

She smiled as a plan occurred to her. It was a risk, of course, but she must focus on the reward.

The following night, Hugh made plans to be much more cautious when it came to socialising. Rachel had not precisely tricked him into dancing. More likely, he had tricked himself, responding to the slightest pressure and giving her what she'd asked for.

It seemed years of avoiding temptation had made him weak when it had finally been presented to him. Now that he could no longer avoid her, he must be careful not to encourage her desire to rekindle what they'd once had.

If she was present tonight, he would know better. Since he was going to a rout, there would be no dancing, which would make it impossible to repeat the mistake of last night.

There would be little of anything, if truth were told. The crowd was shoulder to shoulder, circulating through rooms cleared of furniture. The noise and heat of bodies pressed tight together was oppressive and made him wonder who had ever thought that this was a pleasant way to spend an evening.

He supposed it was too much to hope that she would not be there. In the past, she had been so angry with him that if their paths had crossed she had studiously ignored him and he had done the same to her. But, now that he had revealed some tiny bit of his feelings, she would not leave him alone.

He moved through the crowd, following the eddies and flows of the mass of people packed into the room and having a few short conversations with the men brave enough to approach him. Surprisingly, a few young ladies were foolish enough to meet his eye. It seemed that the single dance on the previous evening had make him a nine days' wonder amongst the debutante set, who were now daring each other to talk to him.

He had Rachel to thank for that, he supposed. When he saw her again, he would tell her not to help him any more.

If. If he talked to her, which he had no intention of doing. It was strange how easily his mind was swayed to do exactly what she wanted him to do. The woman was a witch.

And suddenly, there she was before him, bumping against him as the crowd pushed in on them from all sides. Her gown was the same blue as her eyes, and she smelled of violets and spring time, reviving his spirit, so it was possible to ignore the throng of people around them. 'Your Grace,' she said, stooping to get the fan that had been knocked from her hand by the press of the crowd.

'Allow me,' he said automatically, grabbing it from the floor before she could dip to give him a view of her cleavage. As he picked it up, a piece of paper fluttered out from under it. He grabbed it out of the air and turned it over to read the scrawled note.

Meet me in the library at ten.

When he met her eyes again, she looked properly guilty, as one should when caught setting up an assignation.

He looked at her with narrowed eyes. 'What are you up to now?'

'Nothing,' she said, then added, 'Nothing that concerns you, at least.'

'After last night, you are already meeting another man?'

'Last night?' she said with a laugh. 'Last night was just one dance out of many, Your Grace. And, as I remember, you gave it to me most unwillingly.'

It had seemed like so much more to him. But a sip of water might seem like a torrent to a man in a desert. 'You still should not be meeting alone with men,' he said, feeling as old and starchy as he probably sounded.

She laughed again. 'I will take your opinion under advisement,' she said. 'Although, you are the last person in the world who should caution me on such a thing, given our past history.'

He looked around to make sure that no one had heard, and she laughed again. 'Do not worry about me, Your Grace. Perhaps I am simply doing what my father wishes of me and finding a suitable man to marry.' Then, she snatched back the fan from him and disappeared into the crowd.

The nerve of the woman. She had cornered him on the previous evening, hunting him down like a stag. Tonight, she was willing to throw him away in favour of a stranger. If he had taken the time to watch who else she had danced with on the previous evening, he might have had some idea who she was meeting. But, for now, he was aflame with curiosity.

Or perhaps it was simply jealousy. He was standing silently in the crowd, glaring at anyone who might come near him, unwilling to move forward or back. He checked his watch. It was a quarter to ten.

Unable to help himself, he went in search of the library.

When he arrived, the room was dark and he was alone. Whoever was coming, he had got there ahead of them. The question was, what did he mean to do now? Did he skulk in the corner, as he had during the Perriman incident, and only declare himself at the last minute?

Of course, last time he had not intended to reveal himself at all. He had sat in his chair, quietly horrified, convinced that he was going to be forced to listen to the loss of his love. Instead, Perriman had been an ass and he'd had reason to intervene.

This time, he could not exactly hide himself and wait to see if he was needed. If he witnessed an indiscretion, she would be forced to marry whoever she was with to avoid dishonour. It was better that he make his presence known immediately and put a stop to things before they progressed.

Whoever this suitor was, he would not want to go forward once he knew he was not alone, and it was quite possible that both Rachel and the gentleman would flee back to the main rooms and give up their plan entirely.

He waited in silence as the clock drew closer to ten and, as it struck, the door opened and Rachel entered, closing it quickly behind her. Then, she turned to him and smiled. 'You were early.'

'I only came to keep you from doing something foolish,' he said, suddenly suspicious.

'And what did you think I was doing?' she asked, still smiling.

'Meeting a man unchaperoned.' He stated the obvious.

'Well, I do not see how you could have put a stop to it,' she said, giving him a significant look. 'Here we are.'

'But the message…' he said, confused.

'Was for you,' she finished. 'And you responded, just as I knew you would.'

For a moment, he did not know how to feel. He

was irate, of course. Who would not be, when trapped into a liaison by a duplicitous girl? But there was also a strong and annoying sense of relief that there was no other man she was interested in. 'I should go,' he said, stepping towards the door.

'Surely you can wait for a moment,' she said. 'We have to be careful not to be seen leaving together, as you said the last time we were alone.'

'Have you learned nothing from your time with me?' he asked with a sigh. 'I would think the near disaster of the night my father died would have been enough to teach you the dangers of meeting unchaperoned with men.'

'It taught me the pleasures as well,' she said with a smile that shot through his body like Cupid's arrow. Then, she took a step closer to him, the firelight making her pale skin glow like opal.

'What you remember is a thing of the past,' he said, trying not to think about it. 'We are very different people than we were.'

'Do not tell me I have grown old,' she returned with a moue of displeasure. 'It was not so long ago that you called me the most beautiful girl in London.'

'You are no less lovely than I remember,' he said, and immediately regretted the acknowledgement. It would do him no good to feed the attraction between them. Instead, he must find a way to nip it in the bud. 'I am not blind,' he continued. 'You are one of many pretty girls here tonight. But I am no longer as easily swayed by such things as I was.'

And now he felt guilty for the hurt look in her eye. 'Is there someone else you would prefer to be here with?' she asked, her voice tart. 'If so, tell me now and I will leave you alone.'

He should have lied. Pulled a name from the air and deflated her hopes. Instead, he hesitated, which earned him a smile of triumph from her.

'You are being ridiculous,' he snapped. 'Did you orchestrate this meeting between us so that I might reveal my feelings for someone else? If so, it is unworthy of you. And if you tricked me into coming here so that I might be forced to flatter you…'

'I am not trying to force you to do anything,' she said hurriedly. 'I just wish that you would do what you want to do.'

'And what is that, since you are such an authority on my moods and whims?' he asked.

'You want to be with me,' she insisted. 'You know you do.'

'It is not a matter of wanting,' he said, frustrated. 'We are not children any more and cannot act on each fleeting desire that crosses our minds.'

'Fleeting desire!' she said indignantly. 'Was that all I ever was to you?'

He should declare her correct and storm from the room. A short, brutal lie was the only thing that would close the door to her for ever. But he'd told too many lies in his life already and none, so far, to Rachel. He had no desire to start now.

'You know that is not true,' he said at last, with a

sigh. 'You meant everything to me, and it has been hell on earth to give you up, to search *The Times* each day, expecting to see the announcement that you have married. Though by doing so, you will put an end to the torture.'

And this was what honesty accomplished. Now, she was smiling at him as if his misery was a gift to be savoured. 'That is all I wanted to hear,' she said, beaming at him. Then she crossed the few steps that separated them and launched herself into his arms.

He thought he remembered the feel of her lips, sweet and innocent, on his. But this was different, like being kissed by a stranger. She had been an eager pupil when they had been together last. But today she was the aggressor, pressing her body to his in a way intended to arouse.

He grabbed her arms, intending to push her away. But his grip gentled as his fingers sunk into the soft flesh, and he heard her moan of delight mingling with his own. Her mouth tasted like raspberry, tart and sweet at the same time, her kisses like champagne, going straight to his head and taking him back to a night when the whole world had seemed to wait on the moment she would say yes.

There was no dancing at this party, yet he felt music deep in his bones, light under his skin, singing in his soul and making him sway against her in the most intimate of waltzes. He wanted her, she wanted him and life was simple again.

And then he remembered what awaited him at

home, and the need to be tightly controlled at all times, lest the truth come bursting out. The reality crashed back into him, leaving him panting and angry.

But she felt none of the turmoil he was experiencing. Though the kiss had ended, she was still smiling, rubbing her lips with a fingertip. 'That was even better than I remember.'

'You should not know about such things.' He growled. Who had taught her to kiss like that? Surely not him, for he remembered being able to control himself when he'd been near her.

She shrugged and smiled, and he remembered that she had been the very devil as a girl, totally unaware of what madness she could drive him to. In fact, she had been the one to suggest they meet in private, and he the one unable to resist. She, above all others, had the ability to undo his plans with a flash of skin and a wink.

'It is time for you to go back to the party,' he said, clasping his hands behind his back.

'Perhaps,' she agreed. 'Once you tell me when we can meet again.'

'We cannot,' he replied, trying to bring order to the chaos in his head. 'It is far too dangerous.'

She walked towards the door and, without meaning to, he felt his arms reaching to draw her back. He forced them to his sides before she could turn and see.

As he expected, she spun around and stared at

him, as if expecting to catch the truth in his expression. 'It is just as dangerous to stay apart,' she said, giving him a curious look. 'My father is eager for me to marry and might be arranging a match even as we speak.'

'That is as it should be,' Hugh replied, trying to ignore the jealousy that the suggestion of her marrying raised in him. 'You must marry eventually.'

'If you think so,' she said with a curious look, 'You had best do something about it to secure the desired result for both of us.' Then she listened at the door for a moment before opening it and darting out into the empty hall, leaving him alone.

Chapter Five

The next morning, Rachel woke with a smile after a night of pleasant dreams, all of them about Hugh.

He had been angry with her, of course. But he had responded like a jealous lover when she had given him the slightest provocation. And he had rewarded her with the best kiss since the last one he had given her. Now, the question was how to get another from him.

After breakfast, Rachel's father called her to his study. He was smiling at her in approval, and she wondered at the reason for it. If he had known what she'd been about last night, she was sure he'd have greeted her in a far different manner. Instead, he gestured to the chair in front of his desk and steepled his fingers, looking over them as if he were about to present a gift with his next words. 'There is a new suitor for you. A serious candidate, who meets all the specifications you might raise.' He finished with a nod of satisfaction, as if acknowledging a difficult job well done.

'Who now?' she enquired, running her mind down a column of remembered and rejected names, trying to marshal her features into something other than an apprehensive frown.

'He is five years older than you, good-humoured and sensible,' her father said, ticking off the fine qualities on his fingers. 'And proclaimed by your mother to be quite the handsomest fellow I have talked to. He also has a modest fortune of his own and will inherit enough beyond that to keep you in a manner slightly better than you are used to.'

'Does he have a name?' Rachel asked with a sigh. She supposed the suspense was meant to raise her hopes. But, as with all the other times they had had this discussion, she felt nothing more than prolonged dread. If the man was not Hugh Bethune, then she did not want to hear of him.

'Edward Graham,' her father said with a triumphant wave of his hand.

'Cousin Eddy,' she murmured with a grimace.

'Do not make such a face. There is nothing wrong with the fellow.'

'He used to pull my hair,' she said, covering her curls with a hand.

'That was nearly twenty years ago when you were both children. He has changed much since then, as have you.'

'But that does not mean that we would want to marry,' she said, alarmed.

'He, at least, is willing to consider it. When I die, you will be in his care anyway, if you do not marry first. He is my heir, after all.'

'Stop talking of death,' she pleaded, covering her ears. 'You are not any nearer to that than you were the last time I spoke to you.'

'Actually, I am, if only fractionally. But my current good health does not change the fact that my money and this house will go to him. You owe him respect as the future head of the household. And if you suit, as I think you shall, a marriage will be a damned efficient way to see to your comfort and that of your mother.'

'Efficient,' she echoed with a shudder.

'Do not let your mind be overrun with excuses before you have even talked to the fellow,' her father said with a huff. 'There is no reason that a sensible choice might not also be a happy one. If you allow yourself to think that true romance must be better if it is hopeless, you will never find the happiness that is right under your nose.'

'Thank you,' she replied, her mind racing. She rose from the chair and glanced towards the door. 'And now, if you will excuse me, I must go and prepare...' For something. She was not sure what. But she could not stand to be in this room another minute, listening to reason. And, in one thing at least, her father was right. There would never be a man more 'under her nose' than Hugh, living right next door.

She left the study and went upstairs to her maid. 'Tilly?' she called as the girl put the finishing press on her gown for the evening. 'Do you know anyone in service at the Duke of Scofield's house?'

'Several,' the girl admitted. 'There is Lady Olivia's lady's maid, of course. We share our half days and—'

'What has she told you of the schedule of the house and its master?'

'Only that His Grace is very strict with his sister. She is never allowed out of the house without an escort and there are guards in the yard to prevent her from leaving.'

It confirmed the identity of the gentleman sitting under the tree in the back garden. But it did nothing to help her learn Hugh's plans for the day.

'Does her brother keep regular hours as well?' she asked hopefully.

'He is generally out of the house in the morning to exercise his horse and has his duties in Parliament during the season. But beyond that his nights are a mystery to the household.'

'But he is on Rotten Row in the morning?' she said eagerly.

'I believe so.'

'Then prepare my habit,' she said with a grin. 'Today, I fancy a ride.'

* * *

Rachel arrived at Hyde Park a short while later on a fine mare with a spirited temperament, a footman following behind on a pony as chaperone. The poor fellow was an uneasy horseman, so she left him at the gate, assuring him that she would be perfectly fine travelling the Row without his company.

It was quite likely that he would be able to see her most of the way without following. She was wearing a crimson velvet habit with a high hat trimmed with plumes and rode a horse that was almost blindingly white. She had come here to be noticed and had spared no effort.

Now, she just had to track down her quarry. She brought the mare to an easy trot, slowing to chat with friends as she worked her way down the path until she could see a man on a black horse, riding alone. Although the other riders tended to crowd each other and ride in clusters, there was a ring of empty space around Hugh, as if the rest of the *ton* feared that he had some contagious disease.

She watched him from behind as she worked her way through the trail of carriages and horses, slowly gaining and preparing to make her move. She doubted that he would say anything if she pulled abreast of him. He would be stubborn, she was sure, refusing to acknowledge her, hoping to make her give up and go away.

But he would never fail to help a woman in danger. So she waited until she was clear of other riders, then spurred on her horse and deliberately lost control of the reins. She shot past the Duke at an uneasy gallop, feigning incompetence. In truth, she could have gained control whenever she wanted, for she was an excellent horsewoman. But this was a time when it was better to be helpless than self-sufficient.

She had guessed correctly. She had gone only a few yards when she heard galloping hoof beats gaining on her from behind. A moment later, a strong male hand reached out and grabbed her horse's harness, slowing it to a walk.

'Thank you,' she said, adjusting her hat and raising her eyes to find…

Not Hugh. This man was dark-haired, blue-eyed and vaguely familiar. He smiled at her in a way that was clearly intended to charm. 'If you are afraid that I am going to pull your hair again, you needn't worry. I have not done such a disreputable thing to a girl in at least a year.'

'Cousin Edward,' she said, forcing a smile.

'None other.' He tipped his hat, beaming at her. 'I certainly did not expect to meet you again under such alarming circumstances.'

'Nor did I,' she said, then added a smile and a 'Thank you so much,' after remembering that gratitude for the rescue was necessary.

'You are most welcome. I am very happy to have been of assistance. Allow me,' he said, gathering her reins and handing them back to her. 'Unless you would prefer that I lead your horse for you? I know how upsetting something like this can be.'

'I am…' She bit back the announcement that she was quite capable of handling her own mount, and that the supposed mad gallop had been less than twenty yards in a public park. 'I am all right. But thank you for the offer.'

'At least allow me to ride with you back towards the front of the park. I will accept nothing less.'

So she found herself with an escort after all. And one that would leave her father with the idea that she was in full cooperation with his plans for her. To make matters worse, as they passed Hugh his eyes met hers for only a moment and held a look that implied he knew exactly what she had been about and was more annoyed then impressed.

She smiled back at him, doing her best to pretend that her day had not just gone horribly wrong.

That night, Hugh had promised to attend a ball at the Duke of Haughleigh's townhouse, but he cried off, fearing another interruption of the evening by Rachel. After this morning's appearance in Hyde Park, it was clear that she had learned his schedule and meant to track him through London until he surrendered, which he had no intention of doing.

He could not risk another lapse of judgement like the incident in the library. That had only emboldened her to make that dramatic attempt to attract him this morning. He'd have been worried for her if he had not known that she was an excellent rider, totally capable of regaining control of her own mare.

Another gentleman, not so well-informed, had rushed to her rescue instead. It served her right if she ended up engaged to someone who treated her like the fool she pretended to be. She would be miserable, and he would be...

Not the least bit satisfied by her unavailability. But it was in his nature to be unhappy, so he had best get used to it, and so had she. He stalked to the writing desk and put pen to paper, addressed a missive to the house next door and dropped it in the outgoing post. Then he went back to his room, alone.

The Duke of Haughleigh's ball was an unmitigated failure. The food was excellent, of course, and the music exquisite. Rachel could not imagine a more perfect evening except for one thing—there was no sign of Hugh. She had imagined another brief meeting, and perhaps another kiss.

Instead, she had to pretend to be happy for hours while feeling utterly alone. It was surprising how quickly she had grown used to seeing Hugh and how empty she felt when he was not nearby.

And, though she did not think it possible, when she got home things got worse. She found a letter addressed to her, clearly delivered in the last post of the day. She immediately recognised Hugh's bold hand

and rushed with it to her room, imagining that the words inside would make everything all right again.

Instead, she found a brief, scribbled note.

Rachel,

I know what you were trying to do this morning and I have no intention of letting you make another attempt. Do not look for me again, as I am suspending all social outings until further notice. In the end, you will see that this is for the best.

He had not bothered to sign it—not offered so much as a 'sincerely', much less a declaration of love. Nor had he bothered to begin by calling her his dear.

She crumpled the paper and tossed it into the fire without regret. There was nothing on it that was worth saving to read again. She had been dismissed coldly, brutally, and without reason to hope.

Once the last of the paper had turned to ash, she crept down the stairs and went out of the door to the back garden, wrapping herself in a cloak that hung on a peg by the kitchen door. She could see his window from a place by the back gate, dark as one would expect at nearly three in the morning.

Where was he? Had he stayed home, as his note had implied, or had he gone somewhere that she did not want to know about? Did he have a mistress, as so many men did? Or had he been alone all this time, brooding on the past? He might be up in that room right at that moment, tossing and turning in his bed and thinking of her.

She stooped to the ground and picked up a pebble, switching it from hand to hand and gauging the distance to the glass.

Then she dropped it again. With her luck, she would break the pane instead of drawing him to the window. He might be up in that room, sound asleep and not thinking of her at all. And she might be the biggest fool in all of London for chasing after a man who did not really want her. Though everything about it seemed wrong, maybe she would be better off listening to her father and settling for someone decent but attainable.

Then she heard a sound from the street outside, the irregular step of boots on the cobbles. When she turned to look, it was the man who had been with Lady Olivia at Gunter's. He was staring up at the house, just as she had been, focusing on a window a few doors down from the one that fixated Rachel.

She felt a rush of kinship for the stranger, who thought he was unobserved and showed none of the reserve she was used to seeing in gentlemen, even those who claimed to be in love. She murmured a prayer of apology, for it was unfair to see such naked emotion that she was sure he would have hidden had he known he was observed.

If he was the man Hugh had set to watch his sister, it was pointless of him to pine for her. A duke would never allow an employee to marry into the family. Even worse, she might be in love with another and know nothing of the contents of this fellow's heart, which would likely be broken by her inevitable betrayal.

In this, they had something in common.

She crept to the gate and slipped through it, walking silently down the street to stand at his side.

'Stay away from her.'

He started when he noticed her, turning away from the woman silhouetted in the window above them. 'I beg your pardon?'

'Stay away,' Rachel repeated. 'There is nothing but unhappiness for you if you involve yourself with her, or anyone else in the house. Leave before it is too late.'

Then she followed her own advice and hurried down the walk. When she was almost out of sight of him in the darkness, she darted behind the nearest tree, waiting for him to pass. Instead, she heard his footsteps fading in the night as he walked away in the direction from which they had both come, allowing her to creep back to her own garden and home.

It had been foolish to accost him in that way, and with such a dire warning. But for a moment they had been partners in misery and, if she had dared, she would have thanked him for that. She did not see that unhappiness changing for either of them any time soon.

Chapter Six

The next morning, Rachel came down to breakfast exhausted from a sleepless night, only to find her parents wide awake and smiling at her with approval. 'We heard what you did yesterday and are pleased that you decided to take my wishes to heart with such alacrity,' her father said, nodding as he sipped his coffee.

'Your methods are unorthodox, of course,' her mother said, her voice tinged with concern. 'But I was young once, and understand the desire for a grand passion instead of the sterile way these things can sometimes go...'

'What have I done?' Rachel asked, trying not to sound as tired as she felt.

'You have reintroduced yourself to Edward, of course,' her mother said, much more happily. 'You allowed him to rescue you yesterday morning on Rotten Row.'

'He mentioned it to me last night,' her father added. 'He spoke admirably of your spirit.'

'I am sure you were in no real danger,' her mother observed. 'But it was a rather outlandish way to catch his eye and I am glad that you did not tell us of your plans beforehand.'

'Oh,' Rachel replied, unsure of what more to say. It appeared that her actions had been utterly transparent and yet completely misconstrued. 'I will not do anything like that again,' she promised. Especially as it had been so unsuccessful.

'I believe an offer is forthcoming, and when it arrives—' her father began.

She cut him off. 'I would still prefer to be courted in the usual manner. I do not want to marry a stranger, after all.'

'He is not a stranger,' her father began. 'He is—'

'Perfectly willing to wait, I am sure,' her mother interrupted, much to Rachel's surprise. She smiled sympathetically at her daughter. 'If we speak to him again, we will remind him that it is never a good idea to take a lady for granted. He will woo you as you wish. Won't he?' At this last, she gave her husband a significant look and waited for his assent.

'There is no rush, I suppose,' her father said with a sigh. 'As long as the matter is settled in the next few days.'

'Days?' she said with a gasp.

'Weeks, surely,' her mother said with a calming wave of her hand. 'Let her have the remainder of the season to enjoy. A marriage then will be just as satisfying as one rushed into now.'

Her father sighed again. 'Weeks, then. But do not think you will be allowed to dangle after the man and then cry off. You will be married—if not to him, then someone else. I will not go through another season of waffling.'

It was not actually waffling to refuse proposals if one intended to remain unmarried. But it appeared that would not be an option, nor had she figured out how to convince Hugh to marry her. She would have to work much harder if she did not want to end up wed to Edward.

'And perhaps we shall see Edward at Vauxhall Gardens tonight,' her mother said. 'I wonder if there is a way to inform him of our plans that does not seem too forward?'

'I am sure that is not necessary,' Rachel assured her hurriedly.

'Nonsense. I will send a note, inviting him to accompany us, and we will bring your maid to act as chaperone, should the two of you want to go off alone.'

'Yes, Mother,' she said, wanting to do no such thing. But, if she had the misfortune of meeting her cousin, it would be much better to have Tilly there to prevent intimacy.

'And, above all, you are to stay away from the dark walks,' her mother reminded her.

'What are they?' Rachel said with an innocent blink, then worried that she had feigned too much naivety to be taken seriously, because her mother gave a huff of disapproval.

'Make sure you come home as ignorant as you left, or you will never be allowed outside of this house again.'

That night, as it always did, Vauxhall Gardens dazzled Rachel with its many twinkling lanterns and its novel attractions. But she did not want to admit that the thing that pleased her even more than acrobats who had come all the way from India was the fact that Edward was otherwise engaged and unable to accompany them. She needed a diversion from the prospect of his impending proposal and was ready to lose herself in the night's entertainments.

She was applauding politely, as a pair of boys walked on their hands, when she noticed a familiar face moving through the crowd on the opposite side of the circle. Hugh was there, walking with purpose towards the dark walks at the back of the park. In that space, the lanterns were few and far between, and the entertainments took place between young men and women who had managed to slip away from chaperones and dally on the benches and follies shielded by shrubbery.

Rachel grabbed her maid's hand and yanked her towards the edge of the crowd, calling to her mother that she was indisposed and would be back soon.

When they were out of sight of her parents, she wasted no time in reaching into her purse and producing a gold sovereign, which was more money than Tilly would see in several months. 'I need you to give me some time alone,' she said, holding the coin just out of reach.

'If your father finds out…' the maid said with a worried frown.

'Then he had better not,' Rachel said with a nod. 'And no one need know it is me.' She glanced to her side, where a vendor was selling decorated masks, and reached in her pocket for more coins, purchasing one. 'I promise I will not remove this until I am back.'

'Perhaps, if I turn my head for a moment, you might be lost in the crowd,' her maid said, staring back towards the acrobats.

Rachel dropped the coin into her hand and said, 'Let me borrow your cloak.' Tilly handed it over and she pulled it on, shrouding her body in the plain woollen cape. Then she put on her mask and walked into a swirl of revellers, letting them sweep her down the path towards the dark walks.

Vauxhall Gardens was as it always was, loud and crowded, garish and annoying. But it was the least romantic place Hugh could think of in which to meet Martine Devereaux, which would help to avoid reminding her of old times. He was sure that most men would tell him that a renewed relationship with his former mistress was exactly what he needed to clear his mind of the desire for Rachel. One woman was very like another, when the lights were out.

But that thought was abhorrent to him. Now that he had kissed Rachel again, his mind was too full of her to think of other women. The only thing possible was to suffer the effects in private, as one did with an ague, waiting for the mad recklessness to pass and for life to return to normal.

Martine was walking towards him from across the promenade, an inviting sway in her hips and a smile of invitation on her face. She was beautiful, of course. But tonight he could not remember what had attracted him to her in the first place, other than the assumption that a man of his station would and should have a mistress and that he should try for once to be normal.

When Richard Sterling had taken her away from him, he had gone through the motions of playing the jilted lover, but had been secretly relieved to have rid himself of her so cheaply.

Now, he smiled back at her to prove that there were no hard feelings and kissed her lightly on the cheek.

She gave a coquettish laugh and replied in kind. 'It has been a long time, Scofield.'

'It has indeed,' he agreed. 'Almost a year since you left me. And, from what I hear, you have fared well since our parting.'

'I miss Richard, of course. But my new friend has been generous,' she admitted with another coy smile and a flourish of her hand to showcase the stunning emerald bracelet she was wearing.

'It is good to hear,' Hugh replied. 'For I was wondering if you could do a favour for a generous old friend as well.'

She gave him a sidelong look. 'It would depend on the favour, and the friend.'

'A trifle, really,' he assured her. 'I need a note written in a feminine hand.'

'That is all?'

'A certain young lady of my acquaintance is fixated on an inappropriate suitor. I wish her to believe that the man she is mooning over has another, more persistent female of whom he has not told her. A jealous wife, perhaps.' He shrugged. 'I will leave the details to you. But it should be something that would put her off the fellow, or at least make her suspicious of his motives.'

The courtesan's eyes sparkled with excitement. 'How duplicitous of you. And is this young lady a favourite of yours?'

'She is my sister,' he said, embarrassed. 'She will not listen to me, of course. She is falling for the fellow whom I hired to watch her. Anything I might say will make her more set on him than ever. I learned that much from the elopement of my other sister. But I thought if another woman told her that this Solomon can't be trusted…'

'An anonymous note to terrify her away?'

'Or at least to make her ask difficult questions of the man,' Hugh said with another shrug.

'Say no more. You shall have your note for a kiss and a packet of the biscuits that fellow is selling over there.' She pointed an elegant finger in the direction of the nearest vendor.

'As always, you are a queen amongst women,' Hugh said, raising her hand to his lips and kissing the fingertips in admiration.

Behind him, he heard a strange, sighing sound and turned to see Rachel watching him, in shock. She was wearing a simple cloak over her gown and one of the garish masks that was popular with the throng this evening. It was as if she was there in disguise, although he had no idea who she might be hiding from.

'What are you doing here?' he demanded, feeling as shocked as she looked.

'I was here with my parents and I saw you in the crowd,' she admitted, then looked in horror at Martine, who was still standing at his side.

The courtesan stared back at the girl with interest, and then shot a quick glance at Hugh, giving him a knowing nod. 'If our business is finished, I must be going to write that letter. I will have it delivered to your home. Fare thee well, Scofield.'

'And you, Martine,' he said, then turned back to Rachel. 'Now what is the meaning of following me about London?' he asked, trying to be stern.

'I am not following you,' she said, her eyes darting away as if she feared he would see the truth in them. 'Not all about London, anyway. I did not expect to see you here.'

'Then you will be walking away now,' he said, raising his eyebrow and waiting.

'Who was that woman?' she asked, craning her neck to watch his retreating former mistress.

'That is none of your business,' he replied. 'And where is your chaperone?'

'We decided that we would both have more fun if we separated,' she said with a grin. 'And am I not correctly attired for a night on my own? In this costume, no one will recognise me.'

And yet, he had, without a second glance. 'I think you should go back to your maid,' he said cautiously.

'Not until you tell me who that woman was,' she replied stubbornly.

'An old friend who is doing me a favour,' he said, wondering if she would believe the truth. Then he pulled her down to sit on a bench at the beginning of the dark walk. 'You must stop pursuing me in this way. I cannot give you what you want.'

'Then the least you can do is explain why,' she said, touching his hand.

'I cannot do that either,' he said. 'Just know that things have changed since we were together and what we had is gone.'

'Do you mean that you do not love me? That there is someone else?'

Here again was a moment in which he should lie.

All he had to do was tell her that he no longer loved her, and it would hurt her so much that she would go away. He wet his lips and prepared the words.

'Swear on your honour that you do not love me,' she said. 'Then perhaps I will believe you.'

He shut his mouth again.

She gave him a hopeful smile. 'As long as you do not deny me, I cannot help but hope.'

'And as long as I live, I cannot marry you,' he said in return. 'And on that I can swear. There is no point in hoping. All hope was lost two years ago.'

'Then what can you offer, other than marriage?' she enquired.

'Nothing honourable. Nothing proper.'

'And suppose I do not care if what happens is proper?' she asked.

He should not be surprised. She never had before, when they had loved each other freely and hoped for the future.

Her hand slipped into his, squeezing encouragingly. 'Suppose there is only tonight? The darkness is only a few feet away and will hide all. Suppose I have less than an hour before anyone notices that I am gone? What can you offer me then?'

It was an invitation that he was too weak to resist. The feel of her fingers moving against his, warm and soft, made him imagine how the skin of her throat would feel if he pressed his lips against it. What harm could it do to have one last kiss? He rose and took her by the hand, walking towards the dark walks and intimacy.

Then he froze, the prospect of romance forgotten. His sister was coming out on the same path, led by Michael Solomon. 'What the devil? Olivia? You are not allowed to be out of the house.'

'She should not have got this far. I am to blame for that. But there was no sign of whomever she intended to meet,' Solomon said hurriedly.

It was complete fustian, of course. The man's cravat was undone and there was a flush on his cheek that hinted at mischief.

Olivia had the nerve to lie as well. 'I was not meeting anyone. I came here for my own pleasure.'

'If I were to believe that, it would be even worse,' Hugh snapped, glaring at her. 'That would mean that you have been wandering about London at night with no chaperone at all. We will discuss what you have or have not done tomorrow, when we are both home.'

'And just what are you doing here?' Olivia asked, taking the offensive to draw attention away from her own sins. 'And who is your friend? I do not believe you mentioned where you were going when you left tonight, or where you might be. You only said that you did not mean to come home.'

Behind him, he heard a gasp of alarm from Rachel.

He'd meant nothing by the statement when he'd told the servants not to expect him. Certainly, he'd had no intention of spending the night with Martine.

He had thought to make a late night here and then go on to his private apartments to keep from disturbing the household. But neither had he expected to come upon Rachel or to have Olivia questioning his motives.

He glared at Solomon, trying to gain control of the situation again. 'Take her home immediately and see that she does not stray again.' Then he turned and rushed up the path to find Rachel and explain. But it was too late. She was already lost in the crowd.

Chapter Seven

Rachel pounded her pillow for what seemed like the hundredth time and rolled, with a moan. The sun was rising and the night had been sleepless, filled with self-recrimination.

Hugh had probably slept well in the arms of the exotic woman he had been meeting, who had not worn a mask out of fear of tarnishing her reputation. She probably revelled in the reputation she already had.

Just as bad, she had been near to dragging Hugh into the dark to make love to her. And then he had seen Olivia and she'd been totally forgotten. It was his responsibility to care for his sister until she married, and she doubted he would take a wife until Olivia was safely wed. But how could they ever be together if he refused to allow Olivia to marry?

If she insisted on pursuing him, she should face the fact that she would never be the full focus of Hugh's attention. It was one proof that, as he kept telling her, he was very unlike the man she remembered from years before.

And yet, when he dropped his guard and looked at her, the old hunger was still there. No matter what he said, he still wanted her.

That night, to her relief, Hugh was not at the ball she was invited to. She was still unsure of what she thought about the lady he had been visiting in Vauxhall, if she could indeed be called a lady.

If he had a mistress, or a woman he preferred, it was Rachel's own fault for discovering the fact. He had not asked her to follow him that night, nor had he promised fidelity. In fact, he had been quite insistent that there was no future for them.

Why was it so hard for her to accept?

And now, Edward had arrived, looking every bit the dashing suitor that she did not want to see tonight. He was speaking with her father and bowing deeply over her mother's hand. Then, the three of them turned to look in her direction and her mother was escorting him to her to make sure that the courtship progressed as it should.

'You remember your cousin Edward,' her mother said with a smile large enough to be called a grin. 'Of course, introductions are hardly necessary. I believe you met last in Hyde Park.'

'Of course,' Rachel said, smiling politely and dropping a curtsy. Then she offered her dance card, as was expected.

When her mother was out of earshot, Edward said in a soft voice, 'I am aware that your father has great expectations for a match. But, I must assure you, I am more interested in what you have to say than what he wants. Although I understand it is the practical choice, I am sure we both hope for something more when marrying. Do not feel you have to rush to a decision. I am willing to wait.'

'Thank you for your understanding,' Rachel said, surprised. It was exactly what she had hoped to hear from suitors who had come before him. Thus far, she had been disappointed.

Later, she discovered he danced divinely. He joked with her, and she laughed. When he offered to get her a glass of champagne, she accepted, and allowed him to take her out onto the veranda to look at the stars.

He was polite, pleasant and handsome. He made her laugh. It almost disappointed her that she felt nothing more than friendship when she looked at him. If she was not in love with another, she might have agreed with her father that fondness was a good enough reason to accept an offer.

It was almost reason enough, but not quite. Hugh was not as good a dancer, and it had been years since they'd laughed together. But she could not stop thinking of him. They had been friends once. She simply had to remind him of the fact. Then, he would see that building a life together would help with whatever problems kept him apart from her now.

But at the moment none of that mattered. On the ride home, her parents would demand to know what she thought of Edward and she could not think of anything to say other than the truth. He was an unobjectionable young man. She would happily recommend him to any of her friends. But she did not want to manufacture the passion necessary to marry him, or to lie with him as a wife should.

She was not even supposed to know about the marital act, much less form opinions on men based on her taste for it. And she certainly could not admit to knowledge or preferences pertaining to it when answering her parents.

As expected, when they got into the carriage she was quizzed on how the night had gone. She was evasive. What did one say about a man that had nothing particularly wrong with him? If she did not come up with something when he offered, she would have no excuse at all.

In the end, she announced that they had had a very nice talk but that no promises had been made on either side. She looked forward to seeing him again and to getting to know him better. It was an evasion that would buy her time as she tried to decide what to do about her love for Hugh.

The trip to Vauxhall had been a disaster from start to finish. Hugh had thought that an evening away from Rachel would clear his head and allow him time to settle the growing problem of his sister and her watchdog. Instead, he had managed to stumble into a place where both matters became worse.

Either Martine had meant to hurt him or had totally mistaken what he had asked for when they'd been together. Instead of a letter with a gentle warning from woman to woman that Solomon was already married, she had sent an anonymous threat in red ink that had terrified Olivia's maid and left his sister suspicious but unmoved.

Olivia refused to admit to her feelings for Solomon, so he could not tell whether they were genuine or merely a desperate grasp for any hand that would bear her out of the house. But he could not imagine that she was serious. Had she learned nothing from Margaret's hasty marriage and ban from the premises?

He had lost one sister, and now it seemed he would lose both if he did not lock the doors and guard them himself, like the mad tyrant everyone thought he was.

And, after seeing him with another woman, Rachel was convinced that he had an *inamorata*. It was probably for the best. She was avoiding him again, as she had before. It was simpler that way. If he had no intention of marrying, a future between them was impossible. His love for her had done nothing to change his opinion that his whole family was blighted and it would be better if the line died with him.

And now, after only a day apart, there were ru-

mours that she would be engaged to another very
soon. It seemed that the brief flair of eagerness for
his company had burned out, and she had sought
another the first moment he'd disappointed her. It
should be reason enough for his own feelings to cool
as well.

And yet, it was not. The fact that he had succeeded by hurting her made his own pain greater.
At least, before, he'd known he had one true friend
in the world, even though he could not be with her.
Now he had betrayed her, he was left with no one.

His desk was littered with crumpled paper, notes
begun and discarded to explain that what she had
witnessed was nothing of import. That he had meant
to spend the evening at his club after a late night so
as not to disturb the household. That anything between the courtesan and him had cooled almost as
quickly as it had begun and was long over.

But to write to her would only raise false hopes in
them both. It was better that they parted in anger than
drifted on in false hope with no chance of a future.

His resolve to stay out of her way and mind his
family lasted almost a week. Then he returned to
the house after a night at his club to discover that
his sister was gone again.

This time, according to the servants, she had got
a head start on Solomon, who had taken off in pur-
suit when he had arrived this morning.

He quizzed the staff until he had a good idea of

her destination, then considered. In the past, he had trusted Solomon to bring her back safely. But the way the two of them had looked at Vauxhall left no room for innocence. So Hugh packed a bag and called for his carriage. If he did not act now, he would be tracking the two of them all the way to Scotland before the day was out.

The coachmen took him as far north as they could before stopping for the night. Then they continued in the morning, stopping at each inn on the road until they arrived at the Silver Hare and heard a report of a couple meeting illicitly and sharing a room.

Hugh waited in the coffee room until Solomon and Olivia appeared, looking far too happy to be honest. If Hugh was truly the sort of man given to solving his problems with violence, he'd have called Solomon out, or at least taken him to the coach yard and thrashed him soundly.

But to act in such a way would spread the rumours about Olivia faster than making a discreet exit. So, he sacked Solomon and hauled his sister home in disgrace.

It was time to give up the idea that he could hire a guard for her that she could not outwit or corrupt. Olivia was exhibiting a growing defiance to his wishes and sometimes he wondered if there was any point in trying to control her any more. He was exhausted with worrying what she might do next, and increasingly unable to stop her in her attempts to escape the house. And now he had to worry about the possibility of a bastard.

Should she be with child, he would rush her to the country for her confinement and refuse to bring her back to London next season. It would mean leaving his seat in Parliament empty. And, more difficult still, it would mean no more visits, however brief, with Rachel.

In the short time they had been together again, he had grown used to seeing her. It was a dangerous habit to get into, this taste for forbidden fruit. Maybe it was for the best that he took his sister, retired to his estate and left the city and its many temptations behind.

Almost three weeks had passed since Vauxhall, and when Rachel came down to breakfast both her parents were remarking over an announcement in *The Times.*

'The oldest Bethune girl has married,' her mother said with a smile. 'Her sister has put the announcement in the paper and describes it as a "Scottish wedding".'

'Elopement,' her father said on a grunt. 'There is no hiding the truth.'

'Who is the husband?' Rachel asked, holding her breath.

'A Mr Solomon,' her mother replied, brows knitting. 'I do not know of a Solomon family. Perhaps they are foreign.'

'Don't be ridiculous,' her father said with another huff. 'Scofield would never allow her to associate with foreigners, or anyone else for that matter. This Solomon is probably some common tradesman and she has left the house under a cloud. Scofield would never let her meet a proper gentleman.'

'I am sure they are very happy,' Rachel said, smiling in relief. It seemed that the poor gentleman mooning at the window had succeeded after all.

'Happy to be away from Scofield, more like,' her father said.

'It does not matter, now that she is out of the house,' Rachel said, trying to resist the urge to stand and cheer. Hugh no longer had the excuse that he must for care for his sister and postpone his own marriage. He was free.

There was still the problem of his reputation, of course. But it did not matter to her, as she knew the things said about him were not true. Once they were married, she was sure that society would consider the stabilising influence of a wife as having changed him for the better. Slowly, the past would be forgotten, and she would have the man and the life that she had always dreamed of.

Later, Rachel looked out of her bedroom window, surprised to see Hugh sitting under the tree in the garden where his watchman had often sat. He had a bottle of brandy beside him and, as she watched, he took a long pull on it, tipping his head up and letting the liquor slide down his throat.

Then, as if he truly could feel no pain, he pounded his head on the trunk of the tree behind him.

Unable to help herself, Rachel hurried down the stairs and through the kitchen, out into her garden, then out the back gate and down the path to the Scofield gate, wiggling the loose bolt and letting herself inside so she could rush to sit beside him.

'What is wrong?' she asked, taking the bottle from his hand.

Hugh snatched it back and took another drink. 'Does something have to be wrong for a gentleman to wish a drink in the privacy of his own garden?'

'If that gentleman is you, then, yes,' she replied. 'I have not seen you out here in more than a year, nor do I expect you to be drinking your breakfast.'

'The seat is supposed to be occupied by a guard,' he said with a huff. 'Someone to keep Olivia from running wild. But a fat lot of good it did me to hire Solomon.' He pointed a finger and poked her in the middle of the chest. 'You know as much as I do about how that turned out. You saw them together and warned me. But I allowed myself to become distracted.' He gave her an arch look, as if blaming her for the lapse in attention.

'Your sister married him,' she said, trying not to smile. 'We saw the announcement in *The Times*. And they took the dogs?' she added, noticing the quiet of the empty kennel.

'Gone,' Hugh confirmed with a sweep of his hands. 'All gone. And it is just as well. Those damned pugs hated me even more than my sister did.'

'I am sure she did not hate you,' Rachel assured him, trying to forget the fear in Olivia's eyes the night she had been caught in Vauxhall.

'I gave her no reason to love me,' he said, taking another pull on the brandy bottle. 'But I swear, what I did was for the best. I tried to watch over them both, to keep them safe from the world, and to keep the world safe from them. But it was not enough. They have got away from me, and Lord knows what will happen now.'

Rachel could not stop the laugh that escaped, even though the situation was obviously serious to him. 'You make it sound as if they were dangerous prisoners.'

The silence that greeted this comment made her wonder at the truth of it.

She chose her next words with caution, unsure of what had happened. 'We noticed that Margaret has already married.'

'Eloped,' Hugh corrected. 'With a newspaper reporter who wanted to investigate me.'

'How interesting,' she said, watching for his reaction.

'She lives in a cottage,' he said, shaking his head. 'And claims to be happy. I saw her there yesterday. Olivia was there as well.' The bottle sloshed in his hand as he made an expansive gesture. 'They flaunted the elopement in my face and then Peg's husband, Castell, put me out of the house. There was nothing I could do to stop any of it.'

'I am sure that both girls will be perfectly safe with their new husbands,' she said, giving him an ineffectual pat on the shoulder.

'It was never their safety that was in question,' Hugh replied, staring at her as though he thought her a fool. 'I worry for their husbands. They have no idea what they have married into.'

This idea was too ridiculous to respond to, so she ignored it. 'Now that you no longer have to care for your sisters, you are free to do as you want.'

'I will never be free,' he said, shaking his head.

'You could marry, if you wished,' she encouraged.

'If I wished to marry, you would be the first to know,' he said, looking at her for the first time. 'But I do not.'

'And why is that?' she demanded. 'You are an innocent man, and we both know it.'

'I am not a murderer,' he agreed. 'But I lost my innocence the night my father died and I will never be the man you knew.'

It seemed he'd taken his father's death to heart in a way she could not begin to understand. 'The changes do not matter to me,' she said, taking the brandy bottle from the slack fingers and setting it on the ground.

'You cannot say that without knowing,' he answered, then paused, as if there was some secret he wanted to share.

'Then tell me,' she said, squeezing his hand in encouragement.

'Do you want the truth?' he asked with a laugh. He turned to her, staring into her eyes until her mind went fuzzy and she was lost in the green depths of his, like a swimmer in a stormy sea.

Then he grabbed her, kissing her hard on the lips. His hands on her arms pinned her in place as he ravaged her mouth, his grip so tight that she couldn't have escaped even if she'd wanted to. His tongue thrust into her mouth in a demanding rhythm that was an imitation of something primal and frightening. After this, there could be no denying that he wanted her.

And, Lord help her, she wanted him in return. The feeling was wicked and all-consuming. If he let go of her now, she would sink to the ground and spread her legs for him, letting him teach her the meaning of his kiss under the open sky.

Then, as quickly as it had begun, it was over. He released her and laughed again. 'You want the truth? Well, here it is. I am mad. A madman heading a mad family. My father? My sisters? All mad. And I have no intention of breeding another generation of lunatics to occupy this house and torture each other with their lunacy. Now, give up the hope that there can be any more between us than there already has been.'

Then, he left her alone and returned to his house.

Chapter Eight

Now that Olivia was gone, the house was eerily quiet. He had not noticed how large the place was, nor how empty without even a dog underfoot to break up the solitude. It almost tempted him to reach out to Olivia to ask for one of the infinite number of puppies she needed to find homes for, since David Castell had foisted a mate onto the irritable Caesar the pug.

Almost, but not quite.

Instead, he threw himself into his work and interacted with society only as far as reading the gossip sheets that occasionally crossed his desk.

It appeared from them that Lady Rachel Graham was soon to be engaged to her cousin, Edward. At this news, Hugh could not decide if he was relieved or seething with jealousy. While he had done everything in his power to get her to move on from what they'd shared, that did not mean he had to like it when it happened.

But it did mean that it was probably safe to return

to whatever part of society would have him. Like it or not, after his last repudiation of her, Rachel had selected a more sensible candidate for her hand and he need not fear any more clandestine meetings with her.

Despite that fact, he could not help a feeling of unease as he prepared to go out. He demanded a second shave and went through half a dozen cravats with his valet before declaring himself satisfied. The servant smiled in response, clearly assuming that it was a woman that had him so flustered.

Was it possible to be discomposed by a lack of women? Between the loss of his sisters and the feeling that Rachel was slipping away again, he was at sixes and sevens, unsure of what lay in his future other than silence and loneliness. Tonight, he would haunt the card room and avoid the ladies, ignoring the way they gossiped behind their fans as he walked by, and refusing any false congratulations about his sisters' marriages. And if he saw Rachel…?

Between seeing him with Martine and his drunken ravings in the garden, she was probably no more interested in seeing him than he was in trying to resist her. He must trust that the interludes they had shared recently were a thing of the past. For, no matter what the future held for them, he could not spend the rest of his life hiding away in his rooms.

In Rachel's opinion, her courtship with Edward was going far too well. She had assumed that, by the time things progressed to this point, she would have convinced Hugh that he must act or risk losing her. But with each passing day Edward became more convinced of her eventual acceptance, and she became less convinced that there was a way out of their impending marriage.

If she did not have another offer, her father would not accept a refusal. Perhaps, if she explained to Hugh what was at stake, he would take pity and marry her. He might have a mistress, and a conviction that his family was too unstable to reproduce, but that did not change the fact that he loved her. She would trust in that love as she always had, and she would find a way forward.

That night, they were attending one of the last balls of the season, yet another sign that her time was running out. Edward would be there, of course, and with luck she would see Hugh and could beg him to do the thing that they both wanted.

When she arrived in the ballroom, Edward was there to meet her, bowing low over her hand and claiming the waltz before working his way around the room and helping to fill the dance cards of the other young ladies present. He was a true gentleman, Rachel had to admit. And at least for now, his courtesy gave her time to think.

Hugh was here somewhere. She had heard people talking about him, disapproving as always. She scanned the crowd and saw no sign of him in the ballroom or the dining room. Then she found him on the veranda, standing alone and staring out over the darkened garden.

'I need to talk to you,' she whispered, glancing hurriedly around her to make sure she had not been heard by the other couples enjoying the night air.

'So, speak,' he said without turning round.

'In private,' she whispered. 'Somewhere we can be alone.'

'I do not think that is wise,' he said, still refusing to face her.

'Here, then,' she conceded with a sigh. 'As you may have heard, my engagement is imminent.'

'Congratulations,' he responded mechanically.

'I do not want your good wishes,' she snapped. 'I want help getting out of this.'

'Then, when the gentleman asks, say no,' he said with a shrug as if it made no difference to him how she answered.

She laughed bitterly. 'My father has informed me that a no is not an option. I am to marry by the end of the season, and Edward is my only suitor.'

'He seems like an unobjectionable young man,' he said, but she watched as his fingers that gripped the stone balustrade went painfully white.

'I do not love him,' she said, then waited for a response that did not come.

'Does any of this matter to you?' she snapped. 'Because you cannot have it both ways, you know. I will not be allowed by society to wait in stoic celibacy as you plan to. I have to marry someone, and soon.'

'Then all my blessings will go with you,' Hugh said.

'I want more than your blessing,' she replied. 'I want to know why you are still adamant that we cannot be together, now that your sisters are gone from the house. And do not tell me it is because you are mad. You are as sane as I am.'

She must have been growing louder as she spoke, for he was glancing around now, as if fearing they would be noticed. He looked back at the French doors behind her, which led to a darkened room. He opened them and pushed her through, following her into the room and latching the doors behind them.

Then he turned to face her. 'The problems in my life are far bigger than you can imagine, and they have not been solved by the absence of my sisters. If possible, they have grown worse.'

'Then let me help you,' she said, reaching for his arm.

He stepped back, out of her grasp. 'There is nothing you can do for me. And much that I would do to hurt you by our continued association. Remember the way your mother reacted when we danced?'

'And she was wrong. Nothing came of it,' she said.

'My reputation is the same as it was then,' he said with a sad shake of his head. 'In the eyes of the *ton*, you would be marrying a murderer.'

'But we know it is not true,' she reminded him. 'And that is all that matters.'

'That is but a part of it,' he said. 'My fears for the sanity of the family have not changed. My future is doomed and so will it be for any associated with me. I cannot force you to throw away your life on a hopeless situation.'

'And does what I want have no meaning to you?' she asked.

'You must trust that I know what is best for both of us,' he said in a patronising tone that made her all the more convinced that she was in the right.

Then a plan occurred to her that would solve the problem of Edward and help Hugh as well. He would be angry with her at first, but in time he would see that she was right.

'I am sorry,' she said. 'But you are wrong. And apparently it is up to me to prove it to you.'

She lunged at him, throwing her arms around his neck and planting a kiss on his lips. The suddenness caught them both off-guard and he stumbled back a step before reaching out to hold her and steady them both.

Then he kissed her back. And, as it always did when they were together like this, the world felt right again. His lips moved gently on hers, careful to leave no mark that would betray their activities. His hands stroked her body, grazing the sides of her breasts before gently gripping her shoulders.

She swayed against him, running her fingers

through his hair and loosening his cravat. She wanted to stay like this with him for ever, showered in gentle kisses, feeling the heat of his body and the beat of his heart joining with hers.

Then she remembered that, if things went to plan, she could have this every day for the rest of her life. She just had to be brave and hope that Hugh was the man she knew him to be. So she pulled away from the kiss, gathered her wits, closed her eyes, took a deep breath to steady her nerves and screamed.

When she opened them again, it was to see a look of horror on Hugh's face. The kiss had wiped away all traces of the urbane and bitter peer who had pushed her into the room. It had rendered him young again, as vulnerable as she remembered him.

And he was hurt. He pushed her away from him, as if the touch could burn him, dropping his hands to his sides and clenching his fingers in the wool of his coat tails.

There was a pounding of footsteps in the hall outside and the door was thrown open, a crowd already forming to gawp at her in her disgrace.

She wondered if it disappointed them that there was not more to see. She and Hugh were standing in the room separated by at least five feet. Her clothing and hair were un-mussed, but with Hugh's ruffled hair and loose cravat it would appear something must have been going on. The biggest sign of scandal was the identity of the man she was with and the fact that he would dare be alone with a decent young lady.

The women in the crowd gasped and she heard her mother give a shriek of horror before sinking into a swoon. Edward was there at her side to catch her before she hit the floor. He stared over her head at Rachel, his face a mixture of disappointment and jealous anger.

From behind them, Rachel's father stepped forward and barked, 'Scofield, we will have words.'

Hugh's face darkened in barely contained rage and he turned and directed it at Rachel. 'That will not be necessary.'

Then he stiffly dropped to a knee, as if Napoleon himself had a pistol to his head. 'Rachel, would you do me the honour of becoming my wife?'

If possible, this shocked the crowd even more. Her mother was awake again and weeping openly, as if Rachel had been found dead and not simply compromised.

The rest of the people gathered were murmuring, alternating interest and disapproval. Disapproval of her? She was unaccustomed to anyone noticing her at all, much less having an opinion on her behaviour. And now it seemed she had done something that would make her the talk of the *ton*. Or perhaps it was Hugh they would be speaking of, as always.

'Rachel!' her father shouted from the doorway, obviously irate. 'Answer the man.' His tone made it very clear what the answer must be.

'Yes,' she said softly, staring down at the man before her, clear in his misery. This should be the happiest moment of both of their lives. But somehow she had ruined it, for he looked as though he had been happier when he'd been alone.

Hugh got to his feet. Then, without looking at her, he walked from the room.

She could hear her father calling after him about discussing the settlement, and the muttered reply that they would speak of it in the morning.

Hugh left the room, making his way through the crowd that had gathered and now parted like the red sea before Moses.

Or perhaps it was more like the faithful avoiding a leper. The people around him spurned his gaze, focused instead on the unfortunate girl he had almost ruined.

He wanted to shout at them that he had done nothing wrong. They had been having a simple conversation, in which he had been explaining that there was no way forward for them, when she had forced herself on him and decided without warning to bring the roof down on their heads.

As he thought of what had just happened, he was by turns elated and horrified. Marrying Rachel was all he had ever dreamed of for his future. The thought of her, in his house and his arms, was almost more than he could bear.

But not like this. He did not want to be manipulated into a wedding by society or by her. He had made up his mind long ago that what he wanted and what he could actually have were two different things. Even if he was sane enough to take a wife, and careful enough to avoid getting her with child, there was still the matter of his reputation, which would taint all things between them and make it impossible for her to be seen in society without the censure of women who would never be her equal. She had no idea what she had done in linking her life to his.

But that was his Rachel, always too impulsive for her own good. At one time, it had attracted him to her. Now, it only frustrated him.

He had to get out of here, away from the staring crowds, back to the peace of his own home and the brandy bottle. He drank too much, it seemed, but tonight was not the night to stop.

But now even that was proving illusive. Someone bumped into him, and he looked up, ready to apologise and go around, only to find that the other would not yield. It was the young man who had been dancing with Rachel earlier in the evening. He was glaring up at Hugh in a way he probably thought was intimidating.

Hugh stepped back, ignoring the gasp of the crowd, and staring back in silence to signal that the other man should either speak or move aside.

'You dishonoured Rachel,' the man-child said, refusing to budge.

'Graham. Edward, isn't it? We have not been formally introduced.' He added one part ducal hauteur to his tone and two parts irritated murderer. Normally, it was enough to make even the most persistent fellow back off and leave him alone.

The boy ignored it. 'I demand satisfaction, for Rachel and for the family.'

Hugh rethought his strategy. This was one of those rare situations where he could not just frighten the opposition away. He had to tread carefully to keep from making a disastrous situation even worse. 'It is not your place to demand an apology,' Hugh said in the mildest tone he could manage. 'You are not her father.'

'I am her cousin and Lord Graham's heir,' he countered.

'Well, you have no reason to take exception to me. I am marrying her,' Hugh reminded him, trying not to sound as testy as he felt. 'Beyond that, I do not know what you expect me to do.'

'To trap her into a marriage with the likes of you is no honour,' the boy insisted.

'Trap?' Hugh laughed. If they'd been talking about anyone other than Rachel, he'd have told the fellow the whole truth and withdrawn his proposal on the spot. But, angry though he was at her, he could not do such a thing.

'You are not worthy of her,' Edward snapped, clearly angered by Hugh's lack of response.

'Probably true,' Hugh agreed, trying to mollify him.

'Because you are a murderer.'

At this, the whole room stopped what it was doing and stared in their direction. No matter what everyone thought of the Duke of Scofield, no one had ever said the truth aloud to his face.

This was the moment when he could finally deny it. His sisters were out of his control, after all. Any further deaths need not be laid at his door. There was nothing he could do to protect Liv and Peg, guilty or innocent. He could free himself of the rumours, if he wished.

But he said nothing. Graham's words were an attempt to goad him into a duel, to make him fight to prove his innocence. And if his goal was to save Rachel's reputation, this man, of all people in England, was one that he could not fight.

'Are you not willing to defend your own name? Then how can I trust you to defend Rachel?'

How indeed? He wanted to argue that it had never been his intention to drag her into this, and that in the end they would both be far happier if she thought better of it and refused his proposal.

But Graham took his silence for further insult. 'You have no answer? Let me answer for you.' Then he hauled back his arm and slapped Hugh across the face.

The sound of the blow rung loud as a bell in the silent room. Slowly, Hugh reached to rub the sting out of his cheek, trying not to laugh. It had been a weak attack at best, and he was tempted to announce that

Rachel could have hit him the same way and brought the matter to an end before it had begun.

But the same action from another man was enough to have him arrested for striking a peer. To avoid that, Hugh could probably back down like a coward, apologise for something he had not done and withdraw his offer of marriage. It was clear that, if he did not marry her, Edward Graham would do so. Unless this matter was more about his own pride than it was about Rachel...

Or there was another way out of this. A more permanent way. Hugh could not be forced to deal with what he was not alive to see.

He smiled then, the sort of cold smile that had kept society in terror for two long years. 'Very well,' Hugh said. 'My second will contact you in the morning.'

Chapter Nine

'Were you mad?'

Her father was shouting again.

He had been doing so on and off since they had returned from the ball last night. It was an improvement on her mother, who had retired to her room with a case of the vapours and had been heard weeping for most of the night. Now, she sat in her usual chair across the table, eyes puffed and red, face wan and cheeks hollow, wearing an accusing look to silently remind Rachel that whatever happened now was all her own fault.

'You should have known better than to be alone with him, even for a moment. He is the least trustworthy man in England and you let yourself be taken in by him.'

Rachel let his voice wash over her, leaving her unmoved. She had succeeded in what she'd wished to accomplish, and the rest did not matter.

'It is no wonder that Edward called him out over what he did to you.'

'He did nothing to me,' she said, making her first contribution to the conversation. 'We were alone for but a few minutes.'

'But that is enough to ruin a reputation. And a man with a legacy such as his should know better than to…'

She could not help herself. She laughed. 'You are convinced that a man who would not stop at murder would be halted by fears for my reputation? As if the second sin is greater than the first.'

'You will not be laughing once you are married to the Bluebeard.'

'That is not accurate either. To the best of my knowledge, he has never been married before, much less murdered his wife.'

Her mother let out a wail of misery.

'Do not make light of the situation that you have caused. A good man is likely to die tomorrow, fighting for the honour that you casually threw away. But I suppose you like the idea of men fighting over you.' Her father ended the statement with a derisive huff to tell her what he thought of girls and their foolishness.

'Do not blame me for what Edward did of his own volition,' Rachel answered with a sigh. 'If I had known…' If she had thought he would do something as stupid as issue a challenge, she'd have found another way.

Although she still had no idea what that way

might have been. Perhaps she should have refused him properly before going to talk to Hugh. Then she would not have left him with any hope that she was likely to say yes, had he asked.

For now, she turned to her crying mother, reaching across the table to pat her hand. 'Do not worry about me. I have known Hugh for years and I am not the least bit afraid of him. I know he means me no harm. And I know that, despite what it looks like, he is not a killer. I think he needs me.'

'He is a duke,' her mother reminded her. 'He does not need anyone or anything.'

It was not true, she was sure. No one had ever needed her more. 'Then we should manage well together. Do not waste your tears on me. I am going to be married to a duke. That should be title enough to satisfy anyone's mother.'

Her mother made a scoffing noise and pushed away from the table, storming from the room and leaving Rachel alone with her father.

'That was most unkind of you,' he said, in a mild voice that cut far deeper than any shout.

'I know. But I do not like hearing people speak ill of him,' she said with a sigh, wishing she could make her family understand that this was not the disaster it appeared to be. 'I know he is not who you think he is. And I know that, after a period of adjustment, we will do well together.'

'After he has killed Edward,' her father said with a sneer.

The butler cleared his throat from the doorway and announced the arrival of Mr Graham, who had probably heard them speaking from the hallway, where he'd been waiting.

'Rachel will see him in the drawing room,' her father said, rising to leave the room. Before he went, he turned to her and whispered, 'You have made this mess and now you should be the one to deal with it. Please be kinder to the fellow than you were to your mother.'

As Rachel walked down the hall to meet her cousin, she struggled with what she was expected to say to him that would make any difference.

When she arrived in the room, he turned suddenly, as if she had interrupted his pacing. 'Rachel.' He reached for her, ready to console her.

She did not reciprocate, keeping her own hands firmly at her sides. 'Edward,' she said. 'What have you done?'

'Only what your father was too cautious to do,' he said. 'I do not understand why the family would allow this marriage to go forward when we are all aware of the danger you will be in.'

'I have made my decision,' she said. 'And I am content with it.'

'But what about me?' Edwards replied, giving her a wounded look. 'I thought that I… That *we*…' he corrected, proving that, as she feared, her own place in this was as an afterthought.

'I am not sure what you were expecting,' she lied.

'It was pleasant dancing and talking with you, Edward, but it was never any more than that. I would have explained to you, had you given me enough time. I never expected that you would get yourself into a duel with the Duke. I simply did not think you cared enough about me for that to happen.'

'I cared,' he insisted. But once again he forgot to add the 'about you' that would have made her believe she was anything more than a pawn in his plans to marry by the end of the season.

'If you wait, you will find someone you truly love, and you will see that it is better that way,' she said. 'But, if you do not stop this, someone might end up hurt, or worse.'

'That is the reason behind a duel,' Edward said. 'And I have no intention of crying off.' He was staring at her as if he thought she was simple-minded. 'Something had to be done.'

'And now, something has to be done to save you,' Rachel said, exasperated and starting for the door.

'Where are you going?' Edward asked, stepping in front of the door as if he could somehow control her.

'I am going next door to talk to the Duke,' she said.

'You can't do that,' he insisted.

'Why ever not?' she asked, honestly curious.

'It simply isn't done,' he said. 'There is your reputation to think of.'

'I am engaged to the man,' Rachel reminded him.

'I doubt, at this point, my reputation will get any better or worse based on a single visit.'

'But a duel is a matter between gentlemen and he will not want your interference any more than I do. Leave the details to the seconds,' he warned in the same dark tone he had used when speaking to Hugh last night.

'And if they fail?' she asked.

'Then you don't have to worry about me,' he said with a smile. 'I will prevail against this debaucher and you will have nothing more to fear.' Then he reached for her, as if she was to be the prize at the end of the contest.

She slapped his hands away. 'For the last time, Edward, you have no right to decide my future. You did not offer. If you had, the answer would have been no.' She stepped around him on the way through the door. 'And now, I will go to talk to Scofield about this, whether you like it or not. Hopefully, he will have more sense than you do.' If she could talk Hugh into marriage, perhaps she could talk him out of this duel.

Hugh sat in his desk chair, trying not to think about how the previous occupant would laugh to see him in this situation. The old man had never shown any affection for his children and seeing Hugh's life totally upended would have amused him greatly.

For himself, Hugh was more shocked than amused. But, after the events that had taken place in this very room two years earlier, he told himself he should not be surprised at how quickly things could go very, very wrong. Once again, his life had taken a sharp and unexpectedly disastrous turn and this time he was not going to bother to try and right it.

'I suppose you are wondering why I summoned you here,' he began, feeling unusually pompous as he faced his rather confused brother-in-law sitting in the chair on the other side of the desk.

'I assume it has something to do with Margaret.' David Castell had chosen the obvious answer to the question, and for a moment Hugh wished he could oblige him—and himself—by asking some probing questions about his sister's new life. Was she really as happy as she seemed? Was her pregnancy progressing without any issues? Despite what the man must think, he loved both of his sisters and cared about their welfare.

He would not have sacrificed as he had for them, had he not. He cleared his throat and pushed the distraction aside. 'On the contrary. This is a matter between us.'

'Between us,' Castell repeated, with an expression that clearly said there was nothing between them and therefore nothing to talk about.

'I wish a favour from you.'

'A favour.' Now he was likely thinking of the time that Hugh had sent men after him, threatening him with beatings or worse. Thus far, he had done nothing to earn a boon from this man. Any goodwill received from him would have to be offered on credit.

'This will go quicker if you do not repeat everything I say,' Hugh said with a sigh.

'Very well. What do you wish of me?'

'I need a second,' he said, relieved to have it out.

'A second for what?' asked the other man, still unable to grasp the reason for this requested visit.

Hugh continued as if he had not spoken. 'The challenge was issued last night, so I think some time this week would do. The sooner the better. All told, I should not need more than an hour or two of your time.'

'You mean to duel!' Castell said with an incredulous look.

'It was not my intention,' Hugh assured him. 'I was caught in a compromising situation with a lady and made an offer for her, as was to be expected. But the lady's cousin, who is also a suitor, took exception to that because of my reputation and wants me to pay with my life. You can try to negotiate an end to the thing, but I see no way out other than to go through with it.'

'And this role of your second. Would it not normally fall to a close friend?'

Hugh nodded. 'But since I do not have any friends…'

'No friend at all.'

'You are repeating again.'

'Not verbatim,' Castell replied, then added, 'As a newspaper reporter, words are important to me. And this situation needs all the clarity you can give it.'

'Very well,' Hugh allowed, then continued. 'I cannot think of a single man in London who would be willing to do this for me. In lieu of an acquaintance, I thought family would do just as well. And, since you married my sister and were so interested in my story at the start, I did not think you would mind being there at the finish of it.'

Castell responded to this with silence and raised eyebrows.

'Despite what the world may think, I do not murder every man who stands in my way, and I fail to see how killing this one will make life any easier for me. But if I do not shoot him...'

'Then he is likely to shoot you,' Castell finished.

'And step in as an honourable husband to the young lady at the crux of the matter,' Hugh finished. 'If you would be so kind as to speak to his second and agree on a time and location...'

Now Castell's look had changed to one of speculation. 'In honesty, I cannot say I care whether you live or die. But Peg is quite fond of you, despite all the trouble you caused her, and she would be sad to see you go. If I am to have any peace at home, I must expend at least minimal effort to keep you alive.'

'I expect nothing more from you,' Hugh said with a bitter smile. 'A single attempt at peace-making and an honest review of the events as you witness them will be all that is required.'

'I have never seen a duel before,' Castell admitted. 'It should be quite interesting.'

'I sincerely hope it is not,' Hugh replied, then shuffled through the papers on the surface of his desk to find the calling card that had been left with the butler that morning. 'The other participant is Mr Edward Graham. And here is the name of his second.'

Suddenly, there was a commotion from the hall, and Rachel burst into the study, one step ahead of the butler. The poor servant had given up trying to forestall her and announced her to the room with a sigh of resignation.

'You mean to duel my cousin,' Rachel said, ignoring the other man in the room and glaring at Hugh, as if any of this was his fault and not entirely hers.

'I meant to do no such thing,' Hugh reminded her. 'He was the one who challenged me. If he cannot get the idea out of his head, there is little I can do about it.' He glanced at Castell with a hopeless look. 'It seems our conversation is at an end. Please give my regards to my sister. And apologise to her for the current situation.'

Castell had the nerve to grin at him, as if he had some idea how much trouble a woman could cause, then exited the room with a bow in Rachel's direction before closing the door behind him.

Now, they were alone together again. Hugh stared at her, trying to get the nagging suspicion out of his mind that she was up to no good, as she had been on the previous evening. 'What brings you here?' he asked. 'Haven't you caused enough trouble?'

'I am here to end the trouble, not cause more,' she said, giving him an exasperated look. 'I want to put a stop to this nonsense that you and my cousin are planning.'

'And how do you mean to do that?' he asked, honestly interested.

'By showing you both how silly you are being,' she replied, which was really no answer at all.

'We will meet soon on some stretch of flat ground out of the city, with the intention of shooting each other dead. I cannot imagine a more serious situation than that,' he informed her. 'And do not take it into your own head to come charging between us, risking your own life to put a stop to it.'

'Why would you accuse me of such?' she said. 'I have come here *now* to end it. I do not want to wait until tomorrow or whenever.'

'Has your Edward agreed to that?' he asked with a laugh.

'He is not *my* Edward, and you know he did not,' she said bleakly, sinking into the chair in front of his desk. 'He would not listen to sense.'

'If he does not want to back down, there is nothing to be done,' Hugh said simply, pointing to the door.

'You can cry off,' she pointed out.

'And what, exactly, am I to apologise for?' Hugh asked. 'Proposing to you, or being alone with you? I am heartily sorry for both, but no one wants to hear that.'

Apparently, she did not either, for he saw tears

forming at the corners of her eyes. For a moment, he almost felt guilty about it. But none of that was his fault. It was all down to her. And she would have reason enough to feel sorry once the shooting started.

'I never intended it to come to a duel,' she said in a whisper. 'I had no idea that Edward would behave so.'

It was clear then that she had no idea what she did to men with her attentions, twisting them around her little finger until they no longer knew which direction was up. He was an example of that himself. It almost made him pity her poor Edward. But it did nothing to change their present fate. 'Well, if there is a next time you decide to act rashly, stop and think better of it,' he said with a shake of his head. 'Now, there is only one thing that can be done.'

'And what is that?' she asked eagerly, jumping at anything that could change what was about to happen.

'You can refuse me and marry Graham. That is what he wants, when all is said and done.'

'Is that what you want?' she asked.

'It is the most sensible course of action,' he replied.

'But is it what you want?'

The question hung in the air for a moment as he tried to form the lie that would make her go away. But the words would not come. At last, he said, 'You should go.'

'Is that all the answer you can give me?' she

asked, as if she could press the words out of his mouth when he was no longer sure what he wanted.

'I want this conversation to be over,' he said, sure of that fact at least. 'The duel will go ahead—tomorrow morning, most likely. There is nothing to do to stop it. Now, go back to your house and wait until someone comes to tell you the outcome.'

Chapter Ten

The next morning, Rachel rose and dressed before dawn, then called for a carriage to take her to Edward's rooms. She was waiting on his front steps when his friend called to drive him to the killing ground.

Edward took one look at her and shook his head. 'You are not coming along.'

'If it is my honour that is in question, I do not see why I cannot be there,' she said.

'Because what is to happen is not for a woman's eyes,' he said, huffing the way her father sometimes did when he was tired of reasoning with her.

In response, she laughed. 'You are not the head of the household yet, Edward. If I cannot convince you to call a halt to this mistake, then I mean to be there to see the results of it. It concerns me far more than it concerns you.'

'To me, it is a matter of life and death!' he retorted, amazed.

'It doesn't have to be,' she said, touching his hand. 'It is not too late to cry off. Don't you see that by this duel you are making it worse?'

Her cousin shook his head. 'I will do anything in my power to spare you from this marriage. Nothing can be worse than that.'

'I do not want to be spared,' Rachel announced, hoping that the truth would finally solve everything. 'I love Hugh and want to marry him.'

Apparently, the truth was not as important as what Edward believed, for he was looking at her as if she were an idiot. 'You do not love him, for several reasons. In the first place, you have no idea what it means to love. And in the second, if you did, you would not fix your affections on someone so base and dishonourable as the Duke of Scofield. He is a murderer and a despoiler of women.'

'That is ridiculous,' she said.

'Everyone knows it.'

'They think they know,' she argued. 'But there is no proof that he murdered his father.'

'Then what of Richard Sterling?'

'There is no proof of that either. Only supposition.'

'Then of the last charge, we have proof enough.'

She wrinkled her brow. 'And when has he ever despoiled a woman?'

'You screamed for rescue from him,' her cousin reminded her. 'If that is not reason enough to take up a pistol against him, I don't know what else is.'

'I did not scream for the reason you think I did,' she began, trying to come up with an excuse that would make sense to him. 'I was only startled.'

'You screamed because you were startled?' he asked with a raised eyebrow.

'And I wanted to be discovered so he would be forced to marry me.'

'If you needed to force him to marry you, then he has done something that he shouldn't,' her cousin responded, still stubborn. 'And was refusing to do the right thing in result of it.'

Unfortunately, that was closer to the truth than she would have liked. But explaining the actions of the past would do nothing to stop her cousin's thirst for blood.

'When this is through, you will be free,' he reminded her.

'What does that have to do with anything?' she snapped, confused.

'If you cannot marry him, it will be best if you marry someone,' he reminded her. 'There will be scandal, else.'

'Someone?' she echoed, confused for a moment. Then, incredulous, she asked, 'Is this intended to be a proposal?'

'I'd have got out the words sooner or later,' Edward replied sheepishly. 'We will suit, you know.'

'I do not,' she said quickly. 'And, if you do propose, the answer is no.'

'You cannot refuse,' he said with a grimace. 'You were promised to me. It was all arranged.'

'It was what?' she demanded, shocked. 'I know that my father favours our match. But you told me that there was time for me to make my decision.'

'And I assumed that the decision would be the correct one,' Edward said, spoiling any good opinion she'd had of him. 'I did not think that you would run directly into the arms of the most dangerous man in London.'

'If I did so, it was my choice,' she said. 'That did not mean that you had to challenge him to try and win me back.'

For a moment, he was the cousin she remembered from childhood, uncertain, boyish and in far over his head. Then, he shook off the hesitancy, and obstinacy returned. 'There is no turning back from this. He must pay for what he has done.'

'He has done nothing,' she cried in a burst. 'It was me all along. I tricked him.'

Her cousin stared at her in amazement. 'Why would you do anything so foolish? He is a murderer, several times over. The letter said...'

'What letter?' she demanded.

At first he was silent, looking like a guilty little boy again. Then he blurted, 'A friend informed me that, before I arrived in London, you flirted with Scofield.'

'I danced with him,' she said, then added, 'Once.'

He ignored her excuse and continued. 'This friend

informed me of your betrothed's crimes, enumerating them in a note. It said that he cannot be trusted with women. He abused his sisters horribly.'

'And who is this friend?' she demanded.

'The note was not signed,' he admitted. 'But...'

'You are risking your life and his on an anonymous letter?' she said, her hand to her throat, choking back the horror of it.

'Everyone knows...' he began.

'And everyone is wrong,' she said.

'Then come with me and you will see today,' he said, exasperated. 'Once the pistols are drawn, his true colours will be revealed.' Then he helped her up into the carriage and seated her beside his second, who looked as frightened as she felt at what was about to happen.

The sun was rising as they rode in silence towards an open field on the edge of the city. When they arrived, there was another carriage already waiting. Hugh stood with the man from his study the previous morning. They talked quietly as a nervous surgeon paced in the background.

When he saw her, Hugh's eyes narrowed and he glared at Edward, his sombre expression changing to anger. 'Why is she here?'

'She would not be dissuaded,' Edward said with a shrug, then went back to his own preparations.

While the seconds were examining the pistols, Rachel walked over to Hugh, who was staring past her as if she didn't exist. 'This madness cannot go on,' she whispered to him.

'It is up to Graham to stop it,' Hugh said with the same blasé air that Edward had assumed. 'Apparently, I cannot marry you to satisfy him, and if I give you up I will be fighting your father.'

'I have tried to reason with him,' she said. 'But he received some sort of letter: an anonymous diatribe against you that pushed him to action.'

'While that is very interesting, there is little that we can do about it,' he said.

'There is one thing that you can do for me,' she said. 'Please do not kill my cousin.'

'Do you believe me a killer now?' he asked with a sardonic twist of his lip.

'I believe he is leaving you little choice,' she said. 'All the same, I beg you not to hurt him.'

At this, he laughed. 'Some men, when facing death, look forward to their betrothed praying for their safety. It appears that I am not so lucky.'

Inwardly, she winced. She had forgotten that he was alone in this, and she should be the stalwart on whose faith he could depend. 'I pray for your safety as well,' she said.

'And if you cannot have both, who do you choose?' he asked.

'Don't ask me to do so,' she begged.

'Then stay out of the way,' he said, and stalked towards the seconds. 'The sun is full up. Let us get this over with.'

Now that the moment had arrived, Edward looked like a scared rabbit, as if finally realising the gravity of what he had done. His second handed him a pistol with the quiet assurance that all was in order and that they could begin whenever he was ready.

Edward cast one more look of hopeless desperation in Rachel's direction. Then the two men stripped off their coats and stood back to back.

Hugh did not look at her at all, staring resolutely ahead as they began to pace off the distance. She held her breath as they turned.

There was a single shot.

Edward stood shivering and holding a smoking pistol, obviously appalled at what he had done.

Hugh was still standing as well, a red stain spreading on his left shirt sleeve.

She made to rush to him but the man who was his second held her back. 'He has yet to shoot,' he reminded her in a soft voice.

And now he faced her cousin, who was unarmed and frightened and had wasted his only protection trying and failing to kill her lover.

The time stretched out silently, one agonising second after another, with the blood trickling down Hugh's arm. The expression on his face turned slowly into something strange and terrifying, making him seem every bit the cold-blooded killer that people thought he was. Edward let out a small whimper of fear and closed his eyes.

When it had reached the point where Rachel's own

nerves were stretched to the breaking point, Hugh raised his weapon and fired, deliberately but harmlessly, into the air above his head.

And, for the first time in her life, Rachel swooned.

Being shot hurt like the devil.

But there was so much that was painful about this event that a bullet wound hardly seemed to matter. Rachel had come to him to beg for the life of another man, as if she thought he was some common butcher who would relish taking the life of any fool standing against him. If she did not believe in him, then he was truly alone.

The loss of blood was making him woozy, but he sent the surgeon to deal with Rachel, who had fainted at the sight of her dear Edward being threatened. He sneered at the thought of it then, with as much dignity as he could, sat down upon a nearby tree stump before he swooned himself.

'It is just a graze,' Castell assured him after ripping away his sleeve and making a brief examination of the wound. 'Once we have poured some brandy in you, we will pour some on it and the doctor will bandage you up, good as new.'

'You speak as if you have experience in the matter,' Hugh said, holding out his hand for the flask and taking a deep drink as the revived Rachel was led unprotesting to her cousin's carriage and driven away.

'Some small amount,' Castell admitted without elaborating. 'Now that I am married to your sister,

I have promised to avoid gaining any more knowledge so as not to upset her. This is by far the most dangerous thing I have done in months.'

Did marriage really change a man that much? If it did, he was even more sure than before that he did not wish for it.

'That was a damned cold-blooded thing you did just now,' Castell said. 'There will be an article in my paper tomorrow about a pseudonymous peer facing down his accuser in an honourable fashion and taking no advantage of the unarmed and frightened opponent.'

Hugh sighed. 'I suppose there is no way to avoid the story escaping.'

Castell laughed. 'It amazes me that an innocent man is so intent on keeping the fact a secret. And we know you are innocent, Scofield. After watching you today, I would not say that there is no reason to fear you, but I do not fear that you will murder me or anyone else.'

'I have my reasons,' Hugh replied, concentrating on the sting in his arm.

'Peg feels the same,' Castell reminded him. 'She misses you and is eager to hear of your safety. She was beside herself when she heard of this duel and begged me to see you through it.'

Hugh's throat tightened at the thought of sweet Margaret and her concern for him, comparing it to Rachel and her worries for Graham. 'Tell her I am well,' he said, gritting his teeth in preparation for the surgeon's treatment of his wound. 'And tell her that I will see her soon.'

And with luck he would not see Rachel at all. Now that the deed was done, she was probably congratulating her Edward on his narrow escape, as he suggested a run for Gretna.

The duel had gone better than she had hoped, Rachel reflected. The man she loved was still alive and the matter of Edward's unwanted presence was settled as well. One did not shoot a peer and escape the notice of the law, so he would have to leave London for a while to avoid any prosecution. It was probably better that he be gone before the wedding, as she did not want him standing up in the middle of the ceremony and announcing an impediment or filling her father's ears with foolishness about Hugh's fitness as a husband.

And Hugh… She needed to talk to him as soon as she was able. She had fainted at the sight of the blood on his sleeve and the time he had taken before returning fire. It had been weak of her. As she had insisted on coming along, she should have had the strength to see the duel through to the end. She should have been there to be a comfort to Hugh and to tend to his injuries.

Instead, she had been carted off like an invalid in her cousin's carriage.

Sitting across from her, Edward was silent, finally sobered by what he had done.

'Are you content with the way things went?' Rachel asked, honestly curious to know the answer.

'Honour has been satisfied,' he said in the same ponderous tone he had taken to using when talking to her about her future. 'I will have to flee the city, of course,' he added with a groan of displeasure. 'You can come with me, to Gretna, where we will be married.'

'What?' she asked, sitting up and pulling back until she was in the farthest corner of the carriage, away from him and his second.

'This engagement to Scofield is not really binding. He cannot force you to marry him,' he said with a shrug. 'Since the duel did not go as planned…'

'And just what was the plan?' she asked, liking Edward less with each word he spoke.

'If I had truly prevailed, he would be out of the way permanently. I would still have had to flee the city, of course. But there would be no question of you going with me.'

'Well, there is more than a question on my part,' she said, looking at him in surprise. 'I told you before, I have no intention of marrying you, especially now that you have been foolish enough to embroil yourself in a mess that requires running from the law. Take me home immediately.' She gave the second a pointed look. 'It is your job to see that he acquits himself honourably. And if he, and you, do not turn this carriage towards my father's townhouse, I

shall cry at the first stop—and every one after that—
that I am being kidnapped.'

'That will not be necessary,' the second announced, and signalled the driver to take her home.

'You will regret this decision,' her cousin said in
a dire tone. 'And when you do…'

'*If* I do,' she corrected, 'The matter will be between my husband and me. The fact that you wish
to gloat over a thing which will never come to pass
is all the proof I need that you are not the man you
claim to be. Now, take me home.'

They drove the rest of the way in stony silence.
Arriving at her family's townhouse, Edward put her
out of the coach without offering so much as a hand
to help her to the ground.

She went inside and had to face her parents, who
could not decide whether to punish her for sneak-
ing out of the house or demand a detailed descrip-
tion of the action she had witnessed. She assured
them that, though they might think Hugh was the
last man on earth she should marry, Edward was
most assuredly worse.

Then she went to her room to try and write a letter to Hugh. He deserved some sort of apology for
the way things had gone today, and he certainly was
not going to get it from Edward. In the end, she sent
a carefully worded note enquiring about the wound
in his arm and promising him that he would have no
more trouble from her cousin.

She finished with an assurance that she would be

no trouble either, was eagerly awaiting their wedding and hoped that he would answer to let her know he was recovering.

She signed it with a kiss and a splash of cologne, then dropped it in the pile of outgoing post, praying that it would not be long before Hugh forgave her and accepted that they would finally be together.

Chapter Eleven

To Hugh's surprise, Rachel did not run away after all. She sent him a letter asking about the wound that her idiot cousin had given him, an injury that he'd never have experienced if she had just taken him at his word and left him alone.

The letter was its own kind of hurt, for it reminded him of her behaviour on the day of the duel and how devoted she had seemed to her cousin. If *he* had been fatally struck, would she have spent any time weeping over his grave or would she have sent a weak letter of condolence to his sisters? After a quick read and a moment's indecision, he threw her current note into the fire and refused to answer.

The next day, he received a detailed missive from her father explaining what was expected from him with regard to the impending nuptials. It seemed that they would be proceeding as planned and pretending that the recent contretemps with the younger Graham had never happened.

But, despite following the instructions given, when his wedding day arrived Hugh was no more prepared for it than the day Rachel had tricked him into a proposal.

He had arranged for the special licence requested by Lord and Lady Graham, since he saw no point in having the banns read and allowing three weeks for society to gossip about the match. If it was to be done, better to do it quickly and give the world a chance to forget about it.

He had not bothered to invite his family to gather for what he was sure was a mistake, so he waited alone at the church for Rachel and her parents to arrive with a vicar who looked as frightened by His Grace the Duke of Scofield as the rest of London.

The poor fellow marshalled himself enough to give Hugh a brief lecture on the sanctity of marriage and asked if, under the circumstances, he might wish to confess anything that would clear his mind.

Hugh had not laughed so hard in weeks.

Then Rachel and her parents arrived, hesitating at the back of the church. He turned to stare at her, unable to help himself. She was wearing white today, a muslin gown sprigged with roses the same pink as her lips. And, despite her recent betrayal, he could not help wanting her.

How had something that should be right have gone so very wrong?

He reminded himself that it was never meant to be. She had trapped him into this marriage, which had never been his plan at all. He must not grow soft at the first sight of her, for there was a lifetime of marriage ahead of them and he had to be strong for all of it. There was no triumph here, and certainly no happiness to be gained by this union.

It was supposed to be the happiest day of her life.

But, with her parents' continual fretting and the fact that Hugh had made no effort to contact her, it was hard to keep her spirits up. Still, Rachel was willing to make the attempt, dressing with care and smiling all the way to the church.

Once she got there, things became even more difficult. When they entered at the back of the church, Hugh turned and looked at her with an expression as black as his reputation. It was not at all the sort of welcome she had hoped for, but she must trust that things would be better later, when they were alone.

The vicar glanced from Hugh to her with worried jerks of his head then gestured the Grahams forward so they could begin the ceremony. When he reached the request that any who knew why these two should not be joined speak, he stared out over the empty church, his gaze lingering at the entrance as if he was praying that someone would burst through the front doors and rescue them all.

She let out a sigh of relief as he received no answer, for she had feared that her mother would not be able to resist another fit of vapours. But the moment had passed, and they were getting married, and nothing and no one could stop it now. Only the vows needed to be said and then they would be joined for ever.

Beside her, Hugh looked every bit the dangerous man he claimed to be, simmering with rage at being forced to stand beside her. She would apologise for it later—every day for the rest of her life, if she had to—but if she had not done something she would soon have been standing beside Edward.

The thought made her shudder and the vicar noticed, casting another glance at her groom before asking if there was anything she wished to say.

She shook her head, then reached out to touch Hugh's arm in apology. He flinched and she remembered the wound hidden beneath his coat.

His mouth quirked in a sardonic smile as she withdrew. He then said his vows with a sarcastic snap to his voice, as if to remind her that each promise was delivered under duress.

She should be frightened, she supposed. He was doing his best to scare her out of the church. But she was where she was supposed to be, where he had promised she would be back when they had been in love.

She said her part without flaw, for she had practised it often enough in the quiet of her room, promising to love and to obey, then adding a silent caveat to the Lord that obedience did not mean she would stand for any nonsense in regards to supporting his claim of guilt. Like it or not, she would see to it that this marriage rehabilitated his ruined reputation. Her love would soften him, just as it had before, and the world would see him for the fine gentleman he was.

The moment had arrived for him to kiss the bride. He touched his lips to hers in a kiss that was quick, cold and unlike anything she had received from him before. Then he looked at her with an expression as frigid as his kiss.

'You have what you wanted. I hope you are satisfied with it.' And with that he turned and strode out of the church, not bothering to see if she was beside him.

The wedding breakfast at the Scofield townhouse was a small and dreary affair with only Rachel's parents for company. Neither of them wished to speak to her new husband and he showed no signs of wishing to speak to either of them.

It frustrated her that, though they were far from the *ton* and had only a few footmen for company, he insisted on playing the part that society had set for him, an unrepentant murderer who treated his own family as nothing more than potential victims of his mercurial temper.

Perhaps he thought it would be enough to send her running back to her parents' house. It did not matter to her because she was not afraid of him. Rachel had no intention of leaving now that she had what she'd wanted since the first time she'd seen him. So today, when he scowled, she smiled. He made veiled threats and she laughed as if they were the best jokes she had heard in an age.

In contrast, her parents were clearly terrified for her and for themselves, staring at the wine in their glasses as if they expected every sip to be their last. They spoke to her and each other in hushed tones, shooting glances in Hugh's direction to see if a careless word might be all that was needed to spur him to an act of violence.

She wanted to tell them that everything was going to be all right. For the first time in ages, she knew that her future was going as it should have all along. She had married the man she loved, and the man who she was sure loved her.

But, if that was true, why did he look so angry?

She reinforced her smile and gave her parents a reassuring nod as the meal ended. Hugh's expression was intimidating, of course, but she had seen the man underneath the mask and knew she had nothing to fear.

After pushing his plate aside, the Duke rose, then muttered a brief and cold farewell to her parents before retreating to his study. The minute he was out of earshot, her mother burst into tears. 'We cannot leave you here. We just cannot!' she cried, fumbling in her reticule for a handkerchief.

'If you wish to come home now that you have seen what it will be like, I do not blame you,' her father said in a surprisingly gentle voice.

'I thought that you had consigned me to my fate,' Rachel replied, trying to joke him out of his mood.

'This has gone far enough,' her father replied, now that he could speak freely. 'I know I told you that you must marry before the end of the season. But I am not so hard hearted as to expect you to live with that…' He raised his hand in a gesture meant to convey words he could not bring himself to speak.

She sighed. 'If I need you, which I promise I shall not, you are only one house away.'

'In the house where he murdered his father,' her mother said, then threw arms about her and wept in a way that made the few yards separating their lives seem like hundreds of miles.

'I shall be quite well,' Rachel said, carefully disentangling herself from her mother.

'We shall await your summons,' her mother replied, clearly expecting it within hours.

'I will write to you tomorrow,' she said, offering the only assurance she could think of.

'Or sooner, if you need us,' her father added, offering a brief hug of his own before they departed.

Now she was alone, Rachel went in search of her husband. But when she arrived at the door to the study it was closed against her, and her knock went unanswered. She tried the handle and found it locked, which left her to wonder if he was inside and ignoring her or already in some other part of the house. Perhaps he had even slipped out the back door while she'd been saying goodbye to her parents. She tried not to think of the beautiful woman that he had been meeting in Vauxhall, and the possibility that he might have already escaped his marriage to seek consolation with her.

Really, it should not matter what he did with his life when not with her. Wives were not supposed to make demands on their husband's time, or question how they spent it. If she had married Edward, it might have been no different.

Of course, it would not have hurt quite so much.

She sighed and turned her back on the closed door, reminding herself that there was little to do if he was not ready to speak to her. She must be patient. Now that they were married, she no longer had to worry about losing him. She simply had to wait until his anger cooled, and for that she had all the time in the world.

But that did nothing to fill the empty hours now. Since Hugh had not bothered to introduce her to the staff, she took the liberty of finding the housekeeper and requesting a tour. The woman took her round the house, giving her interesting details about each room before ending at the bedrooms.

The rooms of the two Bethune sisters were unlocked for her and the housekeeper announced, 'We are not sure what to do with the contents. Neither lady has requested her possessions be shipped to her new home, nor has His Grace given us any instructions on what to do with them.'

'I will ask him what he wishes,' Rachel said, wondering if he would give her an answer. Surely he did not feel the need to punish his sisters for abandoning him? It was only natural that they find husbands and start their own lives and families.

'This is His Grace's room,' the housekeeper continued, opening and closing the door before Rachel could get a look inside. It was just as well, for she dared not show any familiarity with the room, though she had been there several times already.

Then the woman opened the door to the adjoining room. 'And this will be yours, Your Grace.' Her knees bent in apology as she said it, for the room she revealed was woefully out of date, the silk on the walls soot-stained and the rug threadbare. 'It has been some time since it was occupied,' she added. 'The last duke prioritised economy over fashion, even while the duchess was alive. And his son...'

'Made no provisions,' Rachel finished for the housekeeper. 'That is all right. Our marriage was sudden, and we have not had a chance to discuss the matter. I am sure whatever you have been able to prepare for me is good enough.' And it was true. For, though the hangings on the bed were out of fashion, they showed no sign of dust, and her maid had already unpacked her trunk and filled the wardrobe with her clothing.

The afternoon passed quickly and when it was time to dress for dinner Rachel chose a sophisticated gown of ruby silk with a bodice that displayed her breasts in a most flattering manner. She added the thick rope of pearls that her mother had given her for a wedding gift and went down to the dining room to greet her husband.

It was then that she learned she would be dining alone, for there was only one place set at the table. She ate in silence, acutely aware of the eyes of the servants as they did their best to impress their new mistress while ignoring the obvious snub from the master.

It made her wonder what it had been like for Hugh's sisters. Had he been taciturn and cold when they'd been in the house, or totally absent? Had they found some way to lighten his mood? Or had his bad humour worn on them, driving them to escape him by marriage?

The meal passed with no sign of her husband, as did the rest of the evening, which she spent in the main salon, just a door down from the shut and locked study door. Was he still inside? she wondered.

She made it as far as the doorway, standing with her hand on the knob and reaching out to knock with the other before losing her nerve and retreating to her bedroom to retire for the night.

Her maid had laid out her best nightdress, one that she had made herself specifically for her wedding night. She had worked on it for weeks, setting each delicate tuck and stitching down the inlays of Brussels lace in lawn so sheer that she shivered just to look at it.

Even when she'd known it was hopeless and they would never be together she had imagined herself wearing it for him. And now, when it appeared that the moment to join with him had finally come, where was he?

She waited for what felt like hours before there was the sound of movement in the adjoining bedroom, the hushed voices of master and valet and the sound of the shutting door as the servant left.

She held her breath then and waited for the knock at her door that did not come.

Did he seriously mean to leave her alone on their wedding night? She could not help herself. She strode to the adjoining door and pounded on it. 'Hugh Bethune, you come in here this instant.'

The door opened with a yank that sent her tumbling into the sudden void. But she couldn't fall, for he was standing there as if he had been listening for her, just as she had for him.

He caught her and set her back on her feet. Then he said, 'What do you want?', biting out each word as if it pained him to say it.

'I should think that would be obvious,' she said, glaring back up at him.

His eyes raked her body, making her aware of the transparency of her gown. 'You mean to tempt me into your bed,' he said.

'Or into yours,' she replied, not wanting to seem too particular after all this time. 'You are my husband now,' she added, in case he had forgotten.

Hugh laughed in response, a sour sound, as if he could barely stand the thought. 'Through no choice of my own.'

'You chose me once and would have chosen me again, given enough time,' Rachel said.

'So that is what you think, is it?' he asked with a bitter smile. 'We will never know for sure, since you tricked me into it.'

'Not intentionally,' she said. It was an exaggeration at best for she had meant exactly what had happened.

'Liar,' he responded.

'I did not do anything that you did not want.'

'I wanted…' He stopped, as if he did not want to admit it, then finished. 'I did not want to marry. Ever. Not to you or anyone else.'

'And now, you are the liar,' Rachel said. 'When we were younger, you asked me dozens of times. You swore that we would be together for ever. But in the end, it was only a mistake that got you to the altar. Do you not understand what that meant to me?'

Now his smile turned cold. 'All young men make promises of that sort and take what they can get from girls who are foolish enough to believe them.'

'That cannot be true,' she said, shaking her head. Her greatest fear, in the last two years, was that what she had trusted as truth was nothing more than the shallowest of lies. But she was sure she was not wrong about Hugh. 'When you kissed me, I felt—'

'You felt what I wanted you to,' he interrupted,

his voice taking on a tinge of impatience. 'When I had no more time for diversions, I left you alone. I wanted you to find someone else. Someone…' For a moment, he seemed to soften, as if he had wished for something better for her. Then he gave a wave of his hand, as if conjuring a man who was all the things he was not and said, 'Someone else. But you have forced me to marry you. Well, I have news for you, Your Grace—you cannot force me to bed you.'

'But…' For a moment, she was not sure she had heard him correctly. Of all the potential issues she had considered, difficulty in getting her husband to bed had never occurred to her. 'You love me,' she said. She had assumed that would be enough.

There was a moment of silence before he laughed. The sound of it ripped across her heart like a dull razor. 'I *wanted* you,' Hugh corrected. 'But there are things I want more,' he said, arms folded across his chest. 'I want the Scofield line to die with me. There will be no children out of this union. And the best way to assure that is to stay away from you.'

Then he tugged the door out of her hand and shut it in her face.

Chapter Twelve

The next morning, Hugh was up at dawn and off to Hyde Park to ride before the rest of the *ton* crowded the Row. He wanted to gallop, to run free of the obstacles weighing him down. And for now the chief problem in his life was still asleep in the room beside his own.

He had not got a wink of sleep thinking of her lying a few yards away in a sheer gown. But he had managed to resist her—for one night, at least—by doing an unspeakable thing.

Now, he had to do it again, and each night for the rest of his life.

At first, he feared that his lies were as transparent as her nightgown and that she must know he loved her like his own life. But after she had gone back to her room and slammed the door between them, he had heard the quiet sobs emanating through the wall, carrying on until nearly daylight. He had lain awake in his bed, fists balled against the urge to comfort her, agonised by her suffering.

But it was fair, wasn't it, that they should both feel the pain of this marriage? If he was to be trapped in a hell of lust-crazed longing, the least she could do was be equally lonely and devoid of hope. If she did not already, she would soon wish to get away from him and might learn to enjoy the advantages of the title without relying on his affection to make their union complete.

One of them was going to the country. She would likely want to stay near her family, who lived in London all year long. But he needed to be near his sisters, at least until he could decide whether the disasters of the past were likely to repeat themselves now that the girls were supposedly happily married. Perhaps they could divide the year, with her in the country for the season, and him in town when Parliament was in session. To be separated from the gaiety of the London season was the last thing any woman would want, and a fitting punishment for the trickster he had married.

Of course, Rachel had never expressed any particular love of parties and balls. When they had first met, she'd enjoyed the garden best of all, and had been fascinated by his stories of life at the manor. And lately, she had been quite insistent that the only thing she wanted was to be married to him.

He gritted his teeth against the sentiment of it. While it was quite nice to have a woman who claimed to love him for himself and not his title, he could not afford to reciprocate that feeling. He was the murderous Duke of Scofield. The mad head of a mad family. There was no room in it for a sweet but devious girl who had loved him before he'd come into his destiny. His mind was made up. He would send her away as soon as he was able.

For Rachel, the sun dawned annoyingly bright and cheerful. Its light streamed through the windows of her new bedroom, brightening the colours on the faded rug and warming the bed linens. It was unfair that in a day starting so auspiciously she should be so lonely.

She had been utterly unprepared for Hugh's denial the previous evening. Of all things she had been sure of, it was that, once they had married, she would be waking in the arms of her lover. She had not imagined in a million years that he would reject the opportunity once the ring was on her finger. A part of her was still convinced that when she saw him again he would assure her that it had all been some terrible joke and that he loved her as much as she loved him.

Instead, she came down to the breakfast room to discover that the Duke had come and gone, off for his usual morning ride. As she had the previous evening, she ate alone, chewing mechanically on food that she had no taste for.

For how long would he be angry with her? Was this a temporary situation, or had he truly felt nothing all this time? He had told her he loved her often enough, right up to the moment his father had died. But had she just imagined the sincerity in his voice when he'd done so? Perhaps she had loved him so much that she'd created his half of the relationship, believing that his ardent actions were a sign of something much deeper.

If that was true, then her parents had been right all along. It would have been better not to feel too deeply when marrying. If she had done so, growing affection for her husband could have come as a pleasant surprise. Instead, like a limb after injury in battle, the love had been amputated from her life, leaving nothing but phantom traces and a strange numbness where her heart should be.

How was she to spend her days living with a man who did not even want to speak to her? Her pride refused to show the servants that she suffered. Nor did she want Hugh to see how much his words had hurt her. There would be no pity on that front, she was sure, so it was best to pretend that she was content until she could find some way actually to be so.

For the moment, at least, she was lonelier than she had imagined it possible to be and the feeling showed no sign of abating. She doubted anyone would have the nerve to visit and offer her congratulations. Even when the old duke had been alive, the Scofield townhouse was not the sort of place that one paid calls on. Now that he was dead, it was as if the house was cursed, and the *ton* avoided it.

But that did not mean she could not reach out to others. Maybe, given a little time, she could coax acquaintances into coming to see her. So, she went to the morning room to write letters.

It seemed pointless to write to her mother, given she was only a few steps away from her, but she had promised a letter to prove that she was not dead. What could she say that did not amount to an admission that they had been right and she totally wrong? She composed a short note to inform her parents that the household was well run, and that supper and breakfast had been excellent.

She pondered for some time what she could say about a husband who refused to be in the same room as her, then decided that a short line assuring them that living with Scofield was different from what anyone had expected summed up her marriage thus far.

After addressing and sealing the note, she decided to write to the two people who should be most welcome in the house, and who probably understood how mercurial Hugh could be. She addressed letters to each of her new sisters-in-law, apologising for their omission from the wedding, inviting them to visit and asking if they wanted to return for the contents of their rooms, and perhaps to visit with their brother.

From what she could gather, they had both departed under a cloud and married men that Hugh did not approve of. But if the poor lovelorn fellow whom she'd seen outside was any indication, Olivia had married in a way that would bring her happiness, if not status. Surely Hugh could not bar them from the family for following their hearts?

Then she thought of the way he had spoken to her the night before and wondered if he had a heart at all, much less the ability to empathise with the loves of others. But, if he was too cold to reach out to his sisters, there was no reason she should not. It had been ages since she had spoken to Liv and Peg and now that they were family she could not allow any estrangement to continue.

When she finished the letters, she took them to the hall to set on the salver that held the outgoing post. Almost as soon as she had laid them down, a footman picked them up and walked not towards the door but down the hall to the study where her husband was hiding.

'What are you doing?' Rachel asked, hurrying after him.

'His Grace has final say in what letters leave the house,' the footman said, puzzled as to why she would want to know.

'Not my letters, surely?' she questioned, giving him the sort of face that she thought a duchess would wear when setting down a servant.

'All letters,' he said firmly, ignoring her authority.

Before he could knock on the study door, she stepped in front of him and pounded against it. 'Hugh!'

The door opened and her husband stood, large and angry, filling the doorframe. 'What now?'

'Now?' she snapped, unable to resist striking back at him now that the opportunity presented itself. 'We have barely spoken since we left the church. Do not dare imply that I am imposing on your time.'

She could see by the look in his eye that he wanted to make some surly comment about the imposition of the marriage itself, but he did not want to air the family laundry in front of a servant. So, he stared at her without speaking, waiting for her to state her business.

'Your footman informs me that I cannot send a letter without your approval.' She took a moment to stare him down. 'I told him that was nonsense and that you have no intention of censoring my correspondence.'

Instead of answering, Hugh held out his hand for the letters and the footman handed them over. He glanced down. 'You are writing to my sisters.'

'I thought someone should, as they did not attend the ceremony or the breakfast. I assumed you would not want them to learn of the wedding by reading it in the newspaper.'

He sighed and looked past her at the footman. 'In the future, we will dispense with the need for me to review the day's post. Let my wife do as she wishes.' Had there been a hesitation before the word wife, or had that been her imagination?

'Very good, Your Grace,' the footman said, taking the opportunity to remove himself.

'Thank you,' she said when the servant had gone, then added, 'Why did you find it necessary to censor the mail before?'

'Maybe I did not want them scattering *billet-doux* about London and then running off with the sort of men they chose,' he said with a shrug.

'Or maybe you caused the elopements by the way you treated them,' she countered. 'One of Edward's complaints against you was the way you treated your sisters.'

'Edward again,' Hugh said with a tone that implied more than two words could hold.

'More accurately, the person writing anonymous notes to him,' she replied. 'That was the person who helped precipitate the duel.'

'It was probably one of my sisters,' he said with surprising conviction.

'Certainly not!' Rachel said, amazed by the accusation. 'I am sure neither of them would want to see you injured, much less killed, if such a plan came to success.'

This was met with a silence that implied that was exactly what he believed.

'They could not possibly hate you that much,' she said, shocked.

'But you do not deny that they hate me,' he replied with a smile. 'We simply disagree on the degree.'

Perhaps he truly was mad. Or perhaps there were

problems in this family that she did not understand at all. 'Then do you not want me writing to them?' she asked, honestly confused by his reticence.

'Do as you please,' he said, his smile turning bitter. 'We both know that you will anyway.' And with that he went back to the papers on his desk, refusing to acknowledge her presence any further.

She glanced down at the letter he was holding, recognising the seal and guessing the contents. 'I am sorry to interrupt you, as you are obviously busy,' she said, trying to restrain her sarcasm, 'But, while I am here, I might as well enquire as to whether we will be attending the Earl of Folbroke's ball. You are holding the invitation in your hand, there. I will accept it for you, if you wish.'

'Who gave you permission to accept invitations?' he asked.

'I assumed no permission was needed, after the discussion on the subject of post we just had,' she said.

'I said you could write to whom you chose,' he responded. 'I said nothing about orchestrating outings.'

'You said nothing against it either,' she pointed out. 'And it normally falls to the wife to accept or refuse invitations.'

'They are only inviting us because they wish to gawk and gossip.'

'Then let them,' Rachel said with a firm smile. 'I would rather that they do it to my face than behind my back.'

'Have you no shame?' he asked, surprised.

'I have nothing to be ashamed of, and neither do you.'

'You cannot know that,' he said.

'Despite the way you are treating me, I know that you are not as bad as people think, and I refuse to live under the shadow of a lie,' she said, praying it was true.

'Very well.' He tossed the invitation in her direction. 'You may go where you want. But do not expect me to come along with you.'

'It will cause even more gossip if I arrive without an escort,' she pointed out.

'Perhaps you should have thought of that before asking to go,' he replied.

'Very well then,' Rachel said, tossing the invitation back to him. 'Neither of us will go, which I suppose is just as you wanted in the first place.' Then she gathered what was left of her pride and left the room.

The nerve of the woman. They had been married only a day and she was already trying to dictate his evenings to him, making him dance to her tune just as she had with the proposal. If he did not stand firm, she would own his life as fully as she possessed his mind. He had not had a decent night's rest since the day he'd met her.

But, if he was honest, there was never any peace when it came to Rachel. He thought about her when he could not see her. He thought about her when he saw her again and, now that they were married, he thought about her constantly.

He drummed his fingers on the table, then looked at the direction on the invitation she had abandoned. Folbroke. He had intended to attend the ball in question even before the wedding. The smoking room would be full of fellow peers willing to trade support for the bill he had been working on nearly all session.

Of course, now that he was married, he would be required to bring his wife. He had wanted to give the world the illusion that he was capable of behaving himself in public for a few hours without running mad and committing mayhem. To leave Rachel at home would lead to rumours that she was afraid to be seen with him or, worse yet, that she was locked in a room somewhere and not allowed out.

He sighed and rang for the butler to summon Rachel back to the study. When she arrived, he had trouble meeting her eyes. Finally, he muttered, 'I have reconsidered the matter of this invitation. We will be going to the Folbroke ball after all.'

'Will we really?' she said. But, rather than enthusiastic, she sounded suspicious.

'You are correct that there is no reason we can't be seen in public together,' he said. 'In fact, there are certain advantages to it.'

'For whom?' she asked, her eyes narrowing.

It seemed that he had not appreciated her cooperation when he'd had it. Now he was going to have to persuade her to do what she would have done willingly a few moments ago. He took a deep breath and began. 'As part of my duties in Parliament, I need to be able to work with the other members.'

'To appear sane, you mean,' she said with a cool smile.

'I do socialise in some limited sense,' he said. 'You have seen me in public recently because of that.'

'And now you need me to accompany you,' she observed, and a calculating look came into her eyes.

'Because it would be strange for me to appear in public without my wife,' he admitted.

Rachel let out a small, triumphant laugh before covering her mouth to stop it. 'Our marriage will give you credibility.'

'Or take it away,' he admitted. 'Depending on how we choose to act when we are together.'

'This is too rich,' she said, her smile softening to something that raised the heat in his blood. 'You need me. I knew you did, of course. But it is nice to see that you are coming to realise it.'

'I need you to do what you have already expressed an interest in doing. It will hardly require effort,' he said.

Rachel pursed her lips and shook her head. 'That was before. Now, the cost of my compliance has increased.'

'What do you want?' Hugh asked, resigned.

'Nothing too onerous,' she said. 'One dance at least. The waltz will be the most appropriate, I think.'

'Very well,' he conceded with a nod.

'And something else,' she said, considering. 'I cannot think what, as of yet. You will have to trust me not to demand the unattainable.'

'I am to trust you,' he said, as sceptical as she had been.

'If we are to have a successful marriage, you will have to learn to do so,' she said, still smiling.

'It was never my plan to be a successful husband,' Hugh reminded her, lest she become too comfortable with his cooperation now.

'Because you do not love me,' Rachel said, and for a moment she looked very near to tears. Then the moment passed and her jaw stiffened as she gave him a brutally efficient smile. 'As my parents continually pointed out to me, love is not necessary to have a successful marriage. It is not as if the oxen tied to the same yoke work together because they love each other. They have simply learned that it is easier for both of them if they are pulling in the same direction.'

Were they to be dumb beasts now, sharing a stable and keeping on their blinders? In his experience, that described the situation of many society marriages. But he had never imagined a situation with Rachel that would be so cold. Still, it was better to have expediency than to be continually at war, and he must learn to accept that it was the best they could manage.

'Very well, then,' Hugh said. 'If you will accompany me to this ball, I will allow you to collect the debt at the time of your choosing.'

'And do not forget the waltz,' Rachel reminded him.

'And a waltz,' he agreed, trying not to smile back at her.

'Very well. We shall go to the ball as man and wife,' she said.

'Duke and Duchess.'

'I will not disappoint you,' she replied. And for a moment he saw a flash of the old, eager Rachel before she smothered it with a frown and hurried from the room.

Chapter Thirteen

Progress had been made.

If she could not get Hugh to admit that their marriage wasn't a mistake, she had at least got him to agree that, in some small way, she could be useful to him. That had to be better than the complete disdain he had showed for her on their wedding night. And it made her feel like less of a fool for wanting to marry him in the first place.

Maybe she had hoped to be lovers when she had dreamed of Hugh in the past. But perhaps there were a host of other feelings involved in the union between man and wife. Helpfulness, for example. Companionship, for another. Her father had spoken highly of security. And, though she had teased her mother about it being better to be married to a duke than a common man, she had to admit that it might be better to be an unpopular duchess than to be no duchess at all. She supposed she would find out the truth of that at the Folbroke affair.

The ball was still a week away and would likely be the last major social event of the season, which meant she would not get another chance to prove to Hugh that she could manage herself in society without embarrassing herself or him. She must make sure that it went perfectly.

This was clearly a case for a new gown, something worthy of a duchess. Rather than moping about the house alone, she decided to spend the afternoon on Bond Street and to visit her *modiste* to discuss a new wardrobe befitting her new title.

Of course, it was not until she arrived there that she remembered she had no idea whether her husband would be willing to pay her bills. Surely one gown would not bother him, especially if it was for an event that he specifically wanted her to attend?

As she was looking through the dressmaker's sketchbook, she felt a strange feeling on the back of her neck and turned to find the other customers looking away quickly as if they did not want to be caught staring. She turned her attention back to the designs, holding first one fabric swatch and then another against the page, trying to decide which would suit.

But it was difficult to concentrate because the silence of the shop made it too easy to overhear the conversations around her.

'The men fought over her.'

'And the murderer married her.'

The comments were delivered in awed whispers

that stopped whenever she looked up. She supposed it was too much to expect that the duel and her sudden marriage would go unnoticed. But she had never imagined that the *ton* would manufacture stories about her, as they had with Hugh.

Now, as she moved about the room selecting laces and trims, the other ladies gave her a wide birth. One woman even exited the shop to avoid her.

Apparently, it was as Hugh had said when he'd first warned her that they could not marry—his reputation had marked her to some as untouchable. He spoke from experience, for he had been going through this for the last two years. He might pretend that it did not matter what people thought of him, but in truth he was the loneliest man in London.

Until now. She must remember to include friendship in her list of marital virtues. Perhaps, once he stopped being so angry, he would remember that they had once been friends.

She smiled to herself and then acknowledged the gossips with another smile and a benevolent nod. Hugh Bethune might refuse to admit to the fact that he needed her. But, now that they were married, he need never be alone in this exile again.

The next morning, Hugh rose, exhausted from another sleepless night. To have the woman of his dreams so close and yet so far away was wearing on his nerves and keeping him awake, wondering if and when he might be too tired to resist.

It appeared sooner rather than later. When he went downstairs, prepared for his morning ride, he found that the servants had saddled two horses and his wife, sleepy but stunning in her red habit, was stumbling down the main stairs to go with him.

'You were not invited,' Hugh said as he turned away from her, reaching for his reins.

'Does one need a voucher of some kind to go to Rotten Row?' she said with false naivety. 'I never have in the past.'

'I meant that you were not invited to go with me,' he amended pointedly before he mounted.

'Then we do not have to ride together,' she said, stepping up on the mounting block that the servants had set for her. 'We will simply ride at the same time.'

'I thought I made it clear that I have no desire to be with you,' he said, hoping that a brutal set down might send her scurrying back to the house.

'On the contrary,' she said. 'You told me you did not love me. And that emotion is hardly required for us to take a ride together.'

'All the same, I prefer...'

'That I remain in the house, as your sisters did?' Rachel finished. 'Well, I prefer that we be seen in public together, to assure the gossips that I have not been murdered on my wedding night. You do not have to enjoy my presence. But, for the sake of my pride, I ask you to tolerate it, at least until the honeymoon is over.'

It was pointless arguing with her, for she had made an excellent point. There was nothing to be done to stop the rumours that were spread about him. But he could take some small measures to minimise gossip about her by proving that their marriage was cordial and she had no reason to fear him. So he set out for the park and she followed a few paces behind him, just as she'd described.

The presence of her there was annoying, like an unreachable itch between his shoulder blades. He wanted to turn around and stare at her, drink in the sight that he had wanted for so long.

Instead, he kept his eyes resolutely forward until they reached the park. Once there, she came up to ride at his side, where she was much harder to ignore.

'I do not come here to converse,' Hugh said through clenched teeth.

'I never said you were required to speak to me,' Rachel replied, giving him a brilliant smile. 'But, should someone notice us, it will seem less odd if we ride together in silence than if I trail behind you, looking abandoned.'

It was probably true. 'Very well,' he muttered. 'Ride where you like.' Then he kicked his horse into a canter.

She followed him easily, laughing as a lock of hair escaped her hat and whipped her face.

Despite himself, he glanced over to admire her, and could not help the way his heart lifted as she kept pace with him. She sat a horse as if she'd been born in the saddle, and he imagined for a moment what it would be like to ride with her through the fields around his estate, stopping to rest under the big oak out of sight of the house…

He pulled up short as his mind wondered what would occur next.

'Is something wrong?' Rachel asked, stopping as well.

'No,' Hugh said, shaking his head to dislodge the strange ideas taking root in his mind. This day was just as he'd imagined it when they'd been together years ago. Then, he had not been able to keep a horse in London, and these rides had been a dream. But in that dream he had always ridden with her.

He had found his dream. Why could he not manage to enjoy it, as a normal person might when having a nice day? Why was he trying so hard to spoil perfection?

He watched as another rider passed them, spurring carefully around and turning his head so as not to acknowledge the presence of a pariah. If the new Duchess of Scofield noticed the snub, she gave no indication of it. Instead, she smiled at the road ahead of them as if she could see a future that he could not.

Perhaps, for just a little while, he could allow himself to ride into that happy place with her. They needn't speak, they needn't plan. They might just exist in the moment.

But then he remembered who he was and what he had done, and the moment was gone.

* * *

When they returned to the house, Rachel retired to her room to change from her habit and revel in her success.

The ride had gone better than she'd expected. Of course, her husband had spoken but a few words. But they had not been particularly angry ones. Eventually, he had accepted her presence at his side and it had been a pleasant morning, though a trifle early for her tastes. She yawned. But pleasant all the same.

'Rachel!'

When she heard the shout, she was rearranging a bouquet of flowers on the bedside table and trying to make the room seem fresher and more cheerful than it was. But the daisies only made the blue walls seem greyer and she had come to suspect that, without a coat of paint and a new carpet, the place was quite beyond hope.

'Here,' she called back. Now she could hear the thumping of determined footsteps coming up the main stairs. Before she could stick her head out of the door, her husband appeared in the doorway, a piece of paper balled in his fist.

'What is the meaning of this?' he demanded, waving it at her but offering no explanation.

She shrugged and waited.

'I opened the morning post and was surprised to find a bill from a Madame Giselle for a new ball gown.'

She nodded. 'I went to Bond Street and bought a gown for the ball you want me to attend.'

'I did not give you permission to spend my money,' he said. 'I did not even give you permission to—'

'Leave the house?' she said with a laugh. 'Do I need your permission for that? I am your wife, not your sister.'

'I...' Was it her imagination or was he blushing? 'I am aware of that.' There was an awkward pause as they both remembered the torrid kisses that they'd shared in the past, and what could happen now if they were so inclined. Then he broke the spell, saying, 'I just thought that we would discuss your spending before you took it into your own hands.'

'At the time, I was unaware we would be discussing anything,' she said, trying not to be annoyed. 'You were not speaking to me, and I was wondering how I was expected to manage the house with no input from you at all.'

'It was never my intention for you to manage the house,' he informed her.

'Because you did not intend to be married to me,' she said with a sigh. 'You made that quite clear on our wedding night. But we are married, and there is no changing the fact, even if you wish it otherwise. And you must admit, it is usually the wife's job to take over the running of the household.'

'That has nothing to do with the purchase of a ball gown,' he pointed out.

'I know I have no right to ask it of you,' she said. 'But I will need some money for personal expenses beyond the household budget.' She did not know why it had not occurred to her that he would be difficult over that. His father had been a well-known skinflint, and it appeared that Hugh had picked up some of his habits. 'If it bothers you, I will send the gown back.'

Of course, then she would have nothing to wear to the ball. She thought for a moment, then went to the dressing table and removed her pearls from the jewellery case. 'If you wish to be reimbursed for the money I spent, I have these. I will sell two or three of them at a time, which will cover the cost of the gown and any other things I might buy. There should be enough pearls to last for several months before anyone notices the difference in the necklace.'

He looked appalled at the suggestion. 'Good God, woman, I am not going to make you sell your pearls to pay for a new gown.'

'Then what do you want of me?'

There was a moment of silence, as if he had trouble finding the right words to answer the question. Then, he took a step in her direction and stumbled over a worn spot on the rug.

'Be careful of that,' she said, too late to do any good. 'The carpet is not in very good condition.'

He glared down at the floor, even more irritated than he'd been before. Then he looked around him, taking in the sad state of the room.

'It has been rather a long time since anything has been done to this room,' Rachel supplied. 'The whole house could benefit from redecoration, but this is the worst.'

Hugh was silent a moment longer. Then he shook his head with disgust and said, 'Take what money you need and redo this room. The rest of the house as well, if you wish. In the future, all bills submitted to my bank will be honoured. Do not concern yourself over the price.'

It was not exactly an apology. Really, it was the opposite of one. It meant that, while he admitted there was a problem, he refused to consult with her about it. He wanted her to change things, but not to bother him. She would have no reason to talk with him at all, which was not what she wanted. All the same, she said, 'Thank you,' and smiled, doing her best to conceal any disappointment she felt.

He nodded and left her to pass the rest of the day in solitude.

But it seemed that he felt some guilt at his neglect of her. That evening, he came to eat in the dining room. And, though he sat at the far end of the table with six feet separating them, it was less like being married to the ghost of the man she had known and more like being with the irritable man he had become.

She helped herself to a thick slice of roast beef from the platter that a footman held for her and said as casually as she could manage, 'It is good to see you, Your Grace. These last nights, I wondered if you might be dining somewhere other than at home.' She held her breath, awaiting the answer.

'I had a cold meal in the study,' Hugh said, focusing on his plate.

'You were not with your mistress, then?' she asked, trying to sound as if it did not matter to her how he answered.

He choked on his wine, then sputtered, 'What made you think that?'

'The woman in Vauxhall was very pretty.' She looked at him over the rim of her glass. 'I assumed that you and she…' She gave a shrug that she hoped was as worldly as that of a duchess's should be.

'It is not your place to assume things about my relationships with other women,' Hugh said in a tone that announced the conversation was over.

He had used the plural and not the singular. Did that mean there was more than one woman to be jealous of? She hoped not, but there was little she could do in any case. She sighed. 'I will not have to assume. I suspect I will be told directly of any relationships you have outside of ours. You are the frequent topic of the *ton* gossips, you know.'

'I take no notice of such things and neither should you,' he said in a firm tone. It was the sensible answer to all gossip, she supposed. But she had already noticed that it was hard to ignore.

A thought occurred to her. 'And I suppose, when you are with your mistress, that you are intimate?'

'This is not something that one discusses with one's wife,' Hugh said, putting down his glass.

'But we are not *actually* husband and wife,' she reminded him.

'We are married,' he reminded her.

'But you have not bedded me,' she countered. 'Because you do not love me. And you say you do not want children.'

He sliced off a large piece of beef and chewed industriously.

'Does that mean that you are in love with her?'

'The two things have nothing to do with each other,' Hugh snapped.

'So you can lie with a woman you do not love,' she said, verifying her suspicions on the subject.

'Rachel,' he said in a tone that warned her to ask no more questions.

She ignored it. 'But, when you bedded your mistress, how did you keep from getting her with child?'

'That should be none of your concern,' he said.

'And yet, it is. I should think that it is a matter of concern for all married women. And it is not as if we are told such things before we are married. I would think that one's husband is the logical person to ask.'

'You would be wrong,' he said, taking a gulp of wine and signalling that the glass be refilled.

'If there is a way that you and I—'

'I thought I made it clear to you that would not happen,' he said, finishing another glass.

'Hypothetically,' she replied, giving him the most innocent look she could muster.

'It requires restraint,' he said through gritted teeth. 'Restraint that I do not believe I would have, should I be with you.'

'Well, that is flattering, I suppose,' she said. Flattering and unsatisfying. But, if he feared a loss of control, perhaps he'd not been as unaffected as he'd claimed to be on their wedding night. She changed the subject. 'I don't suppose you have thought about what we might do together, other than the things that you have already forbidden.'

'What do you know of these other things?' He sounded shocked.

'There are many diversions in London during the season,' she said with a sigh. 'And I am not planning always to stay in the house, as you wished your sisters to. I have done nothing to earn such restrictions.'

'Diversions,' he said with a relieved sigh. 'What do you wish to do?'

'I thought it might be quite nice to go to the theatre.'

'Then go,' Hugh answered without looking up.

'I thought perhaps we could go together. The Duke of Scofield has a box at the Theatre Royal, does he not?'

Hugh grunted in a way that she assumed was an affirmative.

'That is very handy. We will not have to bother purchasing tickets, like my parents do,' she said with a smile.

'I do not like the theatre,' Hugh said gruffly, sounding like a little boy being told to finish his vegetables.

'How strange. I remember you used to quite enjoy plays, although you seldom could afford to go to them.'

'I do not any longer,' he said, focusing on cutting his meat as if the job required supreme concentration.

'Why not?' she pressed, giving no quarter.

'People stare,' he said simply.

It surprised her. For all his claims that he ignored gossip, this was the first evidence she had that he did not like the life that he had chosen for himself. She must proceed with caution or it would sound as if she was blaming him for a very real problem that was only partly of his making. 'I suspect that they will stare even more when I go to the theatre alone.'

'You will not be going alone,' he said sharply.

She smiled back at him. 'I thought not. It is always more enjoyable to go with a companion.'

'I did not mean…' he began, then stopped, as if unsure of what he did mean.

'I am sorry,' she said, surprised. 'Did you mean that I should not go to the theatre? You will have to give me a reason, if you are delivering edicts of that nature. After all, you do not have to keep me con-

fined to the house to keep me from running away. I
came here freely and, if I am to be a prisoner, surely
you can accept my parole and be assured that I do
not plan to leave you in the first week?'

He sighed, then corrected himself. 'I meant you
will not be alone because I will accompany you.'
He tossed his napkin aside and rose from the table.

'Where are you going?' she asked, surprised.

'To dress. There is still time to catch the last act
of whatever it is that you are so eager to see.'

'All right, then. I will meet you in the hall,' she
said, racing for her room to beat him.

As he waited for Rachel to finish dressing, Hugh
was longing for his unfinished roast beef. To admit
to that fact made him seem much stuffier than he
should be at his age. It would be even more churl-
ish to complain about missing his dinner when he
had gone out of his way to avoid it the night before.

But it had not been the food he was avoiding, it
had been Rachel, who seemed to think it was possible to salvage a normal life from what he could
offer. Their marriage was only days old and she was
already tired of the solitude that his life demanded
of her. The only way he could prove to her that isolation was for the best was to subject her to the curiosity of the *ton* until she went fleeing back to her
own sitting room and whatever entertainments she
could find there.

Then she appeared above him, hurrying down the

steps towards the front door in a rustle of gold silk, one hand resting against her bosom, the other trailing elegantly down the mahogany banister, a brilliant smile on her face. His throat tightened as he took her arm and led her to the carriage in silence.

They arrived at his box in the theatre, much to the surprise of the footman left to tend it, and candles were hurriedly lit for them so that it was possible to read the programme.

As he had expected, the audience declared them more interesting than the action on the stage, and stared openly as Hugh helped Rachel to her seat. Women were whispering behind their fans about the new Duchess, probably the fact that, after so much time with him, she was still alive and unharmed.

For her part, Rachel was unmoved by the attention, focusing on the stage where Puck had just turned Bottom into an ass. The only possible sign of nervousness was her hand toying with the long string of pearls that hung about her neck, and her lips moving silently, as if in prayer. Then he looked more closely and could see she was reciting the lines along with the actors.

He smiled. They had entertained each other many times when they'd been younger, reciting Shakespeare back and forth over the garden wall, like Pyramus and Thisbe in this play. And now, here they were again. He searched for the lines and found them ready in the back of his mind, as familiar to him as the woman next to him.

If he made the effort, for a few hours his life could be exactly as he'd imagined it two years ago. He was married to the woman he loved and they were sharing their favourite story. He signalled to the footman to put out the candles, plunging the box into darkness, and making it harder for the crowd to spy on them. Then he settled back in his seat to enjoy the play.

They were quiet in the carriage on the way home. But it was a different sort of silence than Rachel had experienced on the way to the theatre. Then, Hugh had seemed irritable, as if he wished to prove that the evening would be a disappointment. Now, he was satisfied, and she might almost say happy.

'Did you enjoy the play?' she asked.

He grunted again, but a trace of a smile spoiled his attempt at gruffness. 'It has been a long time since we last read it, hasn't it?'

'We must not wait so long again,' she replied.

'Did the crowd bother you?' he asked, looking past her as if afraid to meet her eyes.

'At first,' she admitted. 'But I expect every duchess has to put up with a certain amount of attention.' This had been worse than that, of course. She had heard the whispers when she went to the ladies' retiring rooms during the entr'acte and watched as a few women had deliberately turned away from her. She had ignored it then, and she was not about to allow it to hurt Hugh by association. She smiled. 'But the play was delightful, just as I knew it would be.'

'True,' he agreed, and she felt him relax in his seat.

'And you were there,' she added, smiling. 'I trust that this did not interfere too much with your plans to stay separate from me?'

'It did no harm,' Hugh admitted.

'And do the crowds bother you?' she asked.

'Yes,' he said without hesitation. 'It is tiring to pretend it doesn't matter. And if I am not careful I am goaded into making things worse than they need to be.'

'Like the duel,' she said with a nod.

'Like the duel,' he agreed. 'I did not mean to do anything that would hold you up to ridicule.'

'I have myself to thank for that,' she said with a sigh. 'As you are quick to point out, this marriage was not your plan.'

'There is nothing to be done now,' he concluded with a shrug.

It was not the affirmation she had hoped for, but at least he did not seem as angry as he'd been before. Rachel sighed quietly, tired but satisfied. She could tell Hugh felt the same, for he had stretched his legs across the floor of the carriage until his shoes brushed against her skirts. She did her best to appear relaxed, not wanting to scare him away from what little contact he was willing to give.

And he had already unbent further than she had expected him to. The evening had been so nice that she had almost forgotten how eager he had been to avoid it. Now, he was smiling, probably thinking of the play.

His smile really was beautiful. Perhaps she'd had too much wine tonight, for she could not help herself from sliding across the body of the coach to sit beside him. 'The story was very romantic, was it not?' she asked, unable to stop the silly smile on her face as she stared up at him.

'One might call it that,' he said, his smile fading as he stared down at her, hunger warring with suspicion in his eyes.

'I remember when a few lines of Shakespeare were enough to move you to kiss me.'

'That was a long time ago,' he reminded her.

'You did promise to let me pick my reward for going to the ball.'

'But that has not happened yet,' he reminded her.

'It is not as if I mean to back out of the ball. I have a new gown, after all.'

He sighed in frustration, but there was still a trace of a smile on his lips that encouraged her.

'I am not asking you to love me,' she said softly. 'It is just a kiss. And how much trouble can we get into in a moving carriage?' she added, trying to pretend she did not know the answer.

'I should not find out,' he said, wrapping an arm around her and drawing her close.

A hundred thoughts rushed through her head along with the desire to assure him that she would settle for whatever he would give, and that a peck on the cheek would be enough, if only he would forgive her for this marriage.

Instead, she waited in silence to see what would happen next.

He turned his head to her, touching her chin with a finger to tip her face up to his. 'I should have learned from the past,' he said. 'You would drive a priest to break his vows with that mouth. What hope do I have?' Then his lips came down to brush hers.

It was delicious, but it was not enough. He must have agreed, for he did not pull away. Instead, his arms tightened about her and the tip of his tongue traced her barely parted lips, asking for permission to kiss her properly.

She relaxed into him, opening her mouth with a sigh and inviting him in. The gentle play of his tongue against hers was heaven, making her forget everything else about the past weeks, leaving nothing but the feel of him, finally holding her as he used to.

'And this is why I cannot trust myself around you,' he said, his head sinking to her throat. 'One kiss will turn into a dozen.'

'Will it really be so bad if all we do is kiss?' Rachel asked, gingerly reaching out to stroke his hair as he kissed her.

'You are so hard to resist,' he whispered. 'And in this gown...' His hands reached to cup the under sides of her breasts until the nipples crested above the neckline of her bodice.

'Then don't,' she said, leaning back into the squabs of the seat and letting him take them into his mouth one at a time. He had kissed her there before, when they'd been younger. But then he had been gentle and she had still been learning the pleasures of the flesh.

Tonight, after years apart, he was eager and not afraid to be rough. The stubble on his chin raked against her skin, awakening nerves that she didn't know she had. And when his teeth grazed the hardened buds sensation shot through her body, pooling in her core.

As if he sensed what he needed, his hand dipped beneath her skirts and possessively roved up her thigh until it settled in the delta between her legs. She was on the brink of true happiness. The lightest brush of his fingers would be enough.

Then the carriage drew to a stop and his hand withdrew. The footmen were coming to open the door and she yanked her dress up to cover her breasts and smoothed her hair, embarrassed. Then she remembered that she was married, and their behaviour was not nearly as shocking as it would have been a week ago.

Beside her, Hugh was quiet, his eyes and his mood dark. He followed her into the house, then walked to his room and slammed the door without another word.

Chapter Fourteen

That night, he dreamed of loving Rachel.

That was the problem with a single kiss. It led to more, and yet more, and then a night of dreams and seeking release in solitude that felt lonely instead of satisfying.

He did not want to be alone in his room. He wanted to open the door between the two of them and finish what they had started together. It was why he had avoided marriage in the first place, knowing that he could never be with her in the way he wanted to.

The next day, he skipped his ride and went back to his study, and even he had to admit that he was hiding, just as she had accused him of doing. It seemed his denial of love for her had been only partially successful. If last night's dinner conversation had been any indication, she was already testing the boundaries of what could and could not be done by people who were not in love. He must hope that his noncommittal answers had convinced her that his needs were still being met by a mistress and that he did not require a wife for satisfaction.

He had hoped to distract her carnal curiosity with the trip to the theatre. He had not expected to enjoy it as he had. With the light low in the box, watching the actors on the stage, he had felt human for the first time in ages. For two hours, he had been like any other audience member, wrapped up in the story playing out in front of him.

Then it had ended and they had gone back to the carriage, and in the dim light and close surroundings it had been too easy to forget himself. As they'd kissed, he'd felt human again. It did not matter to Rachel if he was a duke or the keeper of a madhouse. When she looked at him, she saw only the man that she loved.

The temptation of it was both delightful and terrifying. If he recanted his lie and asked her to run away with him, taking nothing but the clothes on their backs, she would do it. They could start again, somewhere else, and leave his problems behind. He could forget it all.

And do what? Even the humblest tradesman had a skill of some sort with which to support his family. But that man could no more become a duke than Hugh could stop being one. He could not imagine a life where he was not Scofield. What would he do with his time?

He could not leave his sisters behind either. If one or the other of their foolish husbands was murdered because of his carelessness in letting them escape, the death would be on his head.

There was a knock on the door and the butler entered with a calling card. 'Mr Solomon to see you, Your Grace,' he said with a slight raise of his eyebrow to indicate that he did not like riff raff cluttering the receiving rooms, even when they were family.

Since Mr Solomon had been an employee before he became a brother-in-law, Hugh could hardly blame him. 'Bring him here.' It would be easier to speak to him in the study and to remove any sense that he was entertaining an equal.

A short time later, Solomon was brought before him and the butler withdrew, shutting the door behind him.

'It surprises me to see you here,' Hugh began, giving the fellow a thoughtful look. It seemed that marriage suited him. The restlessness in his character that had been there before was now missing.

'It surprises me to be here as well. I had thought, now that your sister and I are married, that there would be no more trouble between us.'

Hugh looked up at the man standing in front of his desk, allowing the silence to stretch an awkward few seconds before gesturing to the chair and giving the fellow permission to sit. 'Believe me when I say, Mr Solomon, you are the last thing on my mind.'

'Then do me the courtesy of your full neglect,' the other man responded. 'In short, stop trying to assassinate me.'

'What?' Hugh snapped to alert.

Solomon held his hands out as if shielding himself from objections. 'I know that Margaret and her husband are convinced that it is not you that was behind the murders.'

'How generous of them,' Hugh said in a dry tone.

'But we all suspect that you know more about the identity of the killer than you are saying. If it is someone in your employ, or some acquaintance, or some woman that you feel honour-bound to protect...' He paused dramatically.

Hugh reached for the decanter on his desk and poured himself a brandy. Then he thought on it and poured one for Solomon as well. 'I have no idea what you are talking about.'

Solomon pulled away his cravat and revealed a long, thin bruise about his throat. 'Someone set upon me with a garrotte when I was walking home from my club last night. And, two nights before that, I was very nearly pushed off a bridge and into the river.'

'Someone is trying to kill you,' Hugh said numbly. It was just as he had feared. But there was very little he could do about it now other than to trust that the fellow was fast on his feet.

'That is what I have been trying to tell you,' Solomon said in a tone that suggested he was surprised that he had to explain himself. 'And I want it stopped.'

'It is not me,' Hugh said, and realised that it was the first time he'd spoken those words in two long years. 'It was not me. It was never me.' As the evening with Rachel had been, the phrase was liberating. He felt another dangerous rush of freedom.

'Your lover, then?' Solomon suggested. 'Peg and Castell claim that there was someone else in the house the night that your father was killed. A mad woman.'

'Where did they get that ludicrous idea?' Hugh snapped.

'The housekeeper confirmed it.'

'Then I shall have to have a talk with her about her loose tongue,' he said, letting the old menace creep back into his voice before he could stop himself.

'This is not about what your housekeeper revealed,' Solomon said quickly. 'It is what we learned subsequently. We know you tried to have this woman committed.'

'I… How…?' He shook his head, wondering how they had found information that was safely locked away from the family. 'You are sorely mistaken if you think this has anything to do with…' What was he to call Rachel now? The answer was obvious and yet foreign to him. But was there a need to keep the past a secret?

He took a breath. 'What I am telling you now is not something I wish commonly known. I am now married to the woman who was in this house the night my father died. She had nothing to do with the murder. We were together the whole time.'

'Your wife,' Solomon said thoughtfully. 'That will

be a relief to your sister, who has been beside herself with recent news about you and the fact that she was not invited to the wedding. She has received a letter from the new Duchess and was unsure whether you wished her to answer.'

'I am sorry for that,' Hugh said awkwardly. 'I did not think…' He had not thought that she would want to come back after the way he had treated her. But apparently, he had been wrong.

'I will convey your apologies,' Solomon replied, leaning forward to take another sip of his drink. 'And what about the letters to the asylum that were found?'

'Where and by whom?' Hugh asked, his eyes narrowed.

'Margaret and her husband discovered them in your mistress's apartment.'

He had not kept Martine in almost a year but had not bothered to rid himself of her apartment as the rooms came in handy when he did not want to upend the household by returning home late.

'I suppose I have the annoying scribbler Castell to thank for the discovery of that space?' he said. It was probably unfair of him to speak so of someone who had just helped him, but there had been a time when Castell had been set on proving him a murderer, and the fellow had been a damned nuisance then. 'I suppose this explains why he has left me alone since they married.'

'They were under the impression that you did not

want to see them, since you did not answer Peg's letters,' Solomon replied.

'True as well,' he agreed. 'I have handled things badly.'

'But that does not answer my question about the asylum.'

'I do not think you will like the answer I have for you. And that is that you need look no further than your own house for the one I sought to contain.'

'Olivia?'

'Or Margaret. I have never been sure. Perhaps I should get a cell beside them, for if I were to commit them there would be little reason left to enjoy my life in freedom. But, if you are experiencing mysterious attacks, I would question your wife for the source of them.'

'Then insanity must run in your family, Scofield, for I could not think of a more ludicrous idea.'

'You may think what you like. I know I did not kill our father. And there were only two other people in the house on the night it happened.'

'Three,' Solomon reminded him.

'Rachel had no reason to kill the Duke,' Hugh said. 'More importantly, she did not have time. She was barely in the house before the screaming started.'

Solomon continued to look sceptically at him. 'I do not care what you think. I know your sister as well as my own heart and she is as sane as you or I. Even if she was not, she would never do such a thing.'

'Then Margaret,' Hugh said automatically.

'Have you ever asked her? Either of them?' Solomon asked.

'If they were innocent, I did them no harm in treating them with caution. And if they were guilty?' He tried not to shudder. 'How could I live with their confession? I looked at asylums. But I would not kennel a dog in the best of them, much less send a member of my family. And if they were found and prosecuted...'

Solomon was staring at him as if he could not quite understand what he was hearing. 'You may think this is the logical answer, but that does not make it true. You have to have more evidence than supposition.'

'I have more reason to suspect them,' he said. 'But believe me that, if you love your wife, you do not want to know it. You could not live with yourself if you knew.'

'It would not matter to me,' Solomon insisted, 'Because I am sure that I was attacked by a man. Not even a mad woman would have the strength that I felt in the hands that gripped my throat.'

'If not them, and not me, then who?' Hugh asked, honestly perplexed.

'That is an excellent question,' Solomon replied.

'Until we can find an answer for it, do not travel alone,' Hugh said. 'If necessary...'

'You will set a guard on me?' Solomon finished, amused.

It would be embarrassing for Hugh to admit that he had been thinking something very like that.

'I have been fine thus far,' Solomon replied. 'I will be careful. And if I learn anything I will tell you of it immediately.'

'I suppose I cannot ask for more,' Hugh said, rising and escorting him to the door. 'Send the best to my sister.' *And do not let her kill you,* he added silently.

Then he went back to reading his mail.

Chapter Fifteen

He had been married to Rachel for almost a week, and it seemed they had achieved a sort of truce. In many ways, it was like not being married at all. She did not question his movements, as she had on the night they had gone to the theatre, probably because she had convinced herself that he was still keeping Martine.

He made no effort to disabuse her of the mistake. He dined with her on some evenings and disappeared to his club on others. He told himself that these absences were to remind her that she had no claim on his time or his heart but, though they were painful, they were for his benefit as well. Sometimes, the temptation of having her near grew too much to resist and he had to get out of the house.

He tried not to think about what had happened in the carriage. It had been a lapse in judgement that preyed on his mind, especially when he was alone in his room at night. There was some consolation in the fact that Rachel had moved down the hall to a different bedroom while her room was being repainted. Unless he meant to roam the halls in his nightshirt, she was temporarily out of reach until such time that he could relocate her to his estate in Suffolk and get her properly out of his life.

The thought should have given him some relief. Instead, he felt even more uneasy, as if the distance would be an insurmountable gap and not a day's travel. It was ridiculous. They were married now. And, though it was unwise to see her every day, moving her to the country would not cut her out of his life. He could see her whenever he wished.

But he wished to see her all the time.

Since this had proven unwise, it was best to continue with the original plan.

But she was also very good at making him wonder why he wanted to be with her at all. One day, when he came home from a day spent at the club, instead of the peace and solitude of his study, he found a footman there, balancing on a ladder in the window, waving a tape measure at the curtains.

'What the devil are you doing?' he shouted, causing the man to step back and almost tumble to the floor.

'Her Grace's instructions,' the man said, clinging to the draperies for stability. The old fabric ripped in his hand and the gash left a scar of sunlight across the carpet.

'Rachel!' Hugh shouted. The word and the volume were familiar in his mouth, as was the sense that he was losing control of his life with each day he spent with her.

'Hugh,' Rachel said, appearing in the doorway and smiling at him as if she had just discovered gold. 'You are back so soon.'

'What is going on here?' He gave an expansive wave.

The footman took the gesture as his cue to leave and darted down the ladder, under Hugh's raised arm and out of the door.

As he passed, Rachel snatched a paper and pencil from his hand and looked approvingly at the figures on it. 'We are measuring for new draperies. I was hoping to surprise you,' she said, and her smile seemed to grow even brighter at the prospect.

'I do not like surprises,' Hugh said, giving her his sternest look. 'And I do not like people meddling with my study.'

'You gave me permission to redecorate,' she reminded him.

'Not my private space,' he snapped.

'Your space?' she said, arching an eyebrow. 'Tell me, when was the last time anything was done with this room?'

'I do not know,' he muttered. It was likely the same time as the late duchess's rooms, a renovation so far in the past that there was no way he would remember.

'Then, really, it is not your room at all,' Rachel

said firmly. 'It is your father's study. You just inhabit it.'

'My father is dead,' he said, as if any of them needed to be reminded of the fact.

'And you did nothing to change the room after that happened other than clean up the mess,' Rachel said with a shake of her head.

The answer to that stuck in his throat. He could remember how it had been to be working those first weeks in the shadow of the old man's ghost. To step over the threshold was enough to fill him with dread. But he had bullied through the trouble with raw nerve and brandy, and it had been easier recently. Or so he'd told himself.

She did not give him a chance to affirm or deny but pressed on. 'You are working at the desk where the body was found, walking on the same carpet...'

He remembered his first sight of the room, with the body still slumped over the desk, and tried not to shudder. 'It does not bother me.'

She reached out to the decanter of brandy that sat beside the desk and tipped the liquor in the bottle to show it was three quarters empty. 'Things are well, I am sure.'

'I have more than enough reasons to drink,' Hugh snapped. 'You, for example.'

He had meant to say that the loss of her had made him over-imbibe. But the words had come out wrong. And now the coldness of the first days had returned to her voice and there was a faint sense of injury in her reply. 'Then I will make sure that the decanter is filled when the redecorating is finished. But I assumed with the end of the season you would not be needing the room as much as you have. Unless you mean to continue hiding in it, of course.'

'I was not hiding,' he said, though that was precisely what he had been doing those first days. He could not understand why he was fighting with her now, for he had no reason to love the room—which was not comfortably shabby, as he'd told himself, but dreary, tattered and full of terrible memories.

'Of course not,' Rachel said in a voice dripping with irony. 'On our wedding night, you preferred to eat a cold supper at a dead man's desk than have dinner with me.'

She made it sound foolish and childish and he hated to admit that she was probably right. 'But I am eating with you now,' he said.

'Occasionally. And barely speaking to me when you do,' she snapped.

He had thought the silence comfortable compared to the dinners he remembered with his family, that had been nothing but arguments and threats from start to finish. But, apparently, she was not satisfied with what he could offer. 'At least we were not arguing, as we are now,' he replied.

'We are arguing because I did exactly what you gave me permission to do,' she reminded him.

'Then I should not have given you permission to do anything,' he said, exasperated.

'You are trying to treat me as you did your sisters, controlling every element of my life.' Rachel shook her head. 'Just as your father did to you, when he was alive.'

'I am nothing like my father!' He had not meant to shout. But then, he had not meant to give anyone the impression that his motives were the same as the last duke's. He took a breath. 'It is not my intention to control each element of your life, nor did I mean to be as tight-fisted as my father. I was leaving this room the way it was because it gave me comfort.'

'I do not believe you,' Rachel said, staring into his eyes as if she could see into his soul. 'Perhaps you could fool someone who does not know you as I do. But I know that there was never any comfort in this house when your father was alive and I do not see why you would find it now.'

She was right. Without meaning to, he was becoming his father. Even without the excuse of having two sisters to watch, he was controlling and tight-fisted. He had stayed in this room, drinking to forget the faint stains in the rug and the sight of his father's body. He had allowed his wife to move into a room that was hardly fit for habitation, refusing to see that twenty or more years had passed since it had been cared for.

And, because she was Rachel, she had said not a word of complaint. She had even offered to sell her wedding gift to pay for a new gown.

The wedding gift she had got from her parents.

He had got her nothing. He had not even bothered to send for the jewellery in the lock-room at Scofield Manor.

He could not help that he had been angry at the way this marriage had come about. But, if he expected her to perform the duties of a duchess, the least he could do was treat her better than his father had treated his mother.

He closed his eyes and took a deep breath to clear his head.

'I am sorry. I do not mean to act the way I do towards you. In my sisters' cases, I had reason to be cautious.'

'You were an overprotective brother,' she said, completely misunderstanding the situation. 'But they are both gone now, and happily married. You don't need to worry about them any more.'

'I will never stop,' he said, remembering Solomon's visit and the recent attacks.

'Your diligence does you credit,' she told him, patting him on the arm. 'But things are quite different, now that I am here.'

'Of course,' he said, surrendering with a sigh. 'If you wish to redecorate, then do as you will with this room. It does not matter to me what it looks like.' If it kept her distracted until the end of the season, then he was a fool to complain.

She beamed at him and he felt his heart lurch in his chest. 'You will not be sorry.' Then, before he could stop her, she rushed to kiss him lightly on the lips and ran from the room.

It was wrong to think of each interaction with Hugh as a battle, but Rachel could not help but think that she was winning the war. Though he had been shocked to realise her plans for his study, after she had pressed him on it he had agreed that something needed to be done.

She shivered. Even the thought of what had happened in that room frightened her. It was a wonder that he could think at all when sitting in it.

To break the chill, she stepped out into the garden. There was no reason that she should let the palpable gloom of a single room ruin an otherwise beautiful day. Taking the bench under the oak tree, she tipped her face up towards the dappled light of the sun shining through the leaves and closed her eyes.

Then, from behind her, someone cleared their throat. When she turned to look, she saw a man standing at the back gate, watching her through the wrought-iron bars. They stared at each other for a moment in silence as she tried and failed to remind herself that the correct social response to such rudeness was to cut the stranger dead by ignoring him.

Then, as she watched in shock, he reached through the bars of the gate and manipulated the loose latch, as she had done many times, and let himself into the garden.

'I beg your pardon,' she said sharply, trying to

muster an outraged stare that would put this stranger in his place.

'And I beg yours, Your Grace,' the man said with a deep bow. 'I needed to speak with you, and I could not think of another way to arrange it.'

'Other than to invade my private garden, you mean,' she said, watching uneasily as he approached. He did not look like a threat, and his hands were held in front of him as if to prove his harmlessness.

'Might I have a moment of your time?' he asked, stopping a few feet away in the shadow of a shrub,

'I do not know you, sir,' she said, looking back towards the house for help.

'And if you did, I doubt I would be welcome here,' he admitted. 'My name is Alister Clement, and when I was courting Lady Olivia your husband did everything possible to frighten me away.'

'Olivia is no longer here,' she said, rising to go inside.

'I am aware of that,' he said, taking a step to follow her. 'I feel her absence with each beat of my broken heart. But my concern now is with you.'

'With me?' she said, too surprised to send him away without a hearing.

'Surely you must know of your husband's reputation?' he asked in a disapproving tone.

'Since the accusations are not true, it is not something that concerns me,' she said with a chilly smile.

'You believe your husband is innocent?' Now he was the one who was surprised.

'I do not believe,' she said. 'I know he is innocent.' She gave him what she hoped was a confident smile, pleased to finally meet the gossip that trailed after Hugh with the contempt it deserved.

'How can you be sure?' he said, his head tipped to the side as he awaited her answer.

She considered for a moment. The only truth that mattered was one that she had no intention of sharing with her friends, much less a man that she had just met. Then she realised that there was a truth just as important that he would understand if his heart was as broken as he claimed.

'I know that Hugh is not guilty because I know him. I love him. He is not the man that people think he is. And I will no longer stand for people whispering behind my back, much less walking into my private garden and making accusations.' She smiled at him again, quite proud to be taking the initiative on this rather annoying problem.

'It surprises me that your husband is not equally insistent on his innocence,' Clement said with a sarcastic grin.

'Perhaps he thinks it is beneath him to answer to every person who wants to spout nonsense about his reputation,' she said, hoping that this was the case.

'If it is not him, then he should be conscious of the fact that the murderer is still out there and might strike again.'

She had never thought about that. If the last duke had been a victim, might Hugh be in danger? Surely, if he was, something would have happened by now? 'Thank you for your interest. I will warn my husband of the risk.' She glanced at the gate to indicate that the conversation was over.

'I have not come to warn him,' Clement said with an exasperated shake of his head. 'You are the one that is in trouble. You have married into a cursed family. You need to beware.'

She could not help herself. She laughed. 'Me?' Then she saw Clement's offended look and realised he was probably not used to having his concerns tossed back in his face. She sobered and said, 'I had not thought of that. But I suppose it is possible. I will take care, Mr Clement. And thank you for your warning.'

'If you need anything…anything at all…please come to me. And for the sake of all that is holy, trust no one.' He reached out to her and pressed a calling card into her hand.

'If I need your help, I will write,' Rachel said, glancing towards the gate again. 'And now, I think it wise that you leave before my husband notices your presence.' She did not want to use Hugh as an excuse, but something told her that he would not be happy if he realised Mr Clement had visited.

The fellow nodded. 'Farewell, Your Grace. And take care.' Then he was gone and she was alone again.

Chapter Sixteen

When Hugh returned from his ride the next day, the house was ominously quiet.

When his sisters had first gone, he'd found the lack of noise depressing. But now that Rachel was here the silence worried him even more. She had forgone the morning ride, mentioning that she had other plans for the day, but had given him no hint of what they might be. It likely meant she was up to something that would destroy what little peace he had left.

His fears were confirmed when the servants directed him to the green salon, where his wife was entertaining a gentleman visitor.

A gentleman. And the doors were closed. The jealousy that rose in him was as hot and strong as it was irrational. Unable to help himself, he grabbed the door handles and pulled, barely resisting the desire to shout, *'Aha!'* as he stood in the opening, staring at her and…

He was not sure what he'd expected but it was

certainly not Mr Pilkington of the Bow Street Runners, hat in hand and being served tea by the Duchess of Scofield.

'Rachel,' he said, trying to keep his tone calm, as one would when finding a loved one staring into the teeth of a rabid dog. 'Are you aware who you are entertaining?'

'Of course, darling,' Rachel said, giving him a radiant smile that left him foggy-headed at a moment when he needed all his clarity. 'This is one of the inspectors who was here the night your father died.'

One of the inspectors indeed. He was the chief inspector and the bane of Hugh's existence for weeks afterward, grilling him with endless questions and making it quite clear that the answers were not satisfactory.

'And to what do we owe the honour of this visit?' He directed this to Pilkington, who was staring at him with the same narrowed gaze he had used that night.

'I invited him,' she announced, clearly proud of her brilliant idea. 'I did not think you would mind.'

'Because an innocent man has nothing to fear from the law,' Pilkington announced in a ponderous tone.

'Of course not,' Hugh said, feeling his mouth go dry.

As if she could sense it, Rachel pointed to the tea and said, 'Shall I call for another cup?'

'That will not be necessary,' Hugh said, hoping

the moisture he needed to speak was not sprouting on his brow.

Now she was looking between the two of them, as if trying to draw together a conversation. 'Did you know that Mr Pilkington has no further suspects in the case?'

'I assumed, if he was doing his job and had found the murderer, he'd have informed me of it,' Hugh replied, holding Pilkington's gaze as it narrowed even further.

'There has only ever been one suspect,' the officer replied without blinking.

'And yet, so little evidence,' Rachel said, clucking her tongue. 'You admitted to me now that you had nothing other than Hugh's presence in the house on that night.'

'And the threat he made at dinner,' Pilkington added.

'But people have often heard him make such threats before and since. And yet, the people he threatened are still alive,' she pointed out.

'Not all of them,' Pilkington responded. 'Two were murdered.'

'And could that not also be a sign that someone is trying to make him seem guilty?' she suggested in a reasonable tone.

At this, Pilkington was silent, probably too busy locked in his staring contest with Hugh to give an answer. Fortunately, two years as a duke had given

Hugh the gift of the superior glare and he used it now to the best of his ability.

'Was that a nod, Mr Pilkington?' Rachel asked innocently. 'I don't believe I heard your answer.'

'It is possible,' the man admitted slowly. 'Other explanations are far more likely.'

'But the likely answer is not always the right one,' she said, helping herself to a biscuit.

'Do you have some evidence to support your claim?' Pilkington enquired with a raised eyebrow.

'No more than you have to support yours,' she replied.

'But I have an instinct about such things,' the officer admitted.

'And I am a woman, and therefore naturally intuitive,' Rachel replied with a smile. 'I am also married to the man you are accusing and can find no trace of murderous violence in him.'

Hugh was tempted to announce that she must not be looking very hard. If he could have murdered the Runner with a glance, it would have been done long before now.

'While a witness to his character is a fine thing, it surprises me that His Grace cannot speak for himself,' Pilkington replied with a note of triumph.

'Because I do not dignify such things with a response,' Hugh said automatically.

Rachel sighed. 'I said he was not violent. But I will admit that he is stubborn. Or perhaps there is another name for it, when one is a duke. Imperious?' She considered the word as she sipped her tea.

Now the Runner looked at Rachel with the same penetrating stare he had tried on Hugh. 'You are disappointing me, Your Grace. I had come here in hopes that you had some information to give me pertaining to the murders. But it appears that is not the case.'

'And I invited you here to see if you had any real information about the crime. Apparently, that is not the case.' She gave him another of her perfect smiles. 'You may finish your tea. But, after that, this interview is at an end.' Then she gave him a look that was as worthy of any duchess he had seen, staring the man down until he bolted his tea and excused himself.

When they had heard the front door close and were sure that the Runner was gone, Hugh closed the salon doors and exploded. 'What was the meaning of that?'

'I wanted to know if the Runners had more information than they'd let on.' She smiled as she refreshed her cup. 'Even after two years they have no idea who committed the crime because they are too intent that it is you.'

'I am aware of that,' Hugh said. 'And just what made you think I would allow that man back into this house?'

'I did not think I needed permission to entertain a guest,' Rachel said, batting her lashes at him and feigning innocence.

'Pilkington was not a guest. He is an adversary,' Hugh said with a snarl.

'Not mine,' Rachel replied, her expression unchanged. 'And I had your interests at heart when I summoned him. I think it is for the best that we know what he knows. And that he knows that I do not believe a word of the speculation about you.'

'I do not need your help,' Hugh said firmly. The last thing he needed was for her to upset the delicate balance of his life and set the Runners looking for the real murderer.

'That is the problem with you, Hugh,' she said, shaking her head. 'You are always so insistent that you do not need me, and yet you do. You are certainly not doing that well on your own.'

'I was doing perfectly well,' he insisted, trying to remember a moment of the last two years that had felt like a success.

'Well, then, I am not,' Rachel said with a stubborn set of her chin. 'I cannot bear to see you suffer as people accuse you of something you have not done.'

'I am not suffering,' he insisted. But why did his voice not sound as confident as it once had?

'Do not lie to me,' she said, her eyes as narrowed as the Runner's had been. 'It is bad enough that you will not tell the whole truth. But do not lie.'

'I am used to things the way they are,' he said. That was much closer to the truth, at least.

'Like the study,' she said. 'But things are changing. Your sisters are both gone and I am here now.

And I refuse to allow you to take the blame for something you did not do.'

'I would rather it be that way than that they learn the truth,' Hugh said with a sigh.

'And what is that, exactly?' she asked. 'We both know that you are not the killer. But that means that the real murderer is walking free and might kill again.'

'I will not let that happen,' Hugh said, knowing he had already tried and failed.

'If he has killed one Duke of Scofield, he might kill another. Now that I have you, I cannot bear to lose you.' The sudden impact as she threw herself into his arms was enough to knock the wind from his lungs.

He held her. How could he resist? It had never occurred to him that she might be worried for him, and it was both flattering and inconvenient. He did not want her exposing truths that were better buried in an attempt to help him. 'Do not worry about me,' he said, kissing the top of her head and pausing to inhale her scent. 'I have lived this long without incident. I doubt there will be a problem in the future.'

'But what if there is?' she insisted. Her face grew pale, and her eyes seemed to grow even larger as she looked up at him. He was losing himself in the blue depths of them, and in her fear that something might happen before they had spent even one night in each other's arms.

'It will be all right,' he assured her, dropping his

head and kissing her. And for a moment everything was all right. She nestled close to him, the gentle friction of her body raising old memories of passion-drugged hours and the future he had promised her when he'd still had hope.

Her arms stroked his back, both comforting and seeking comfort. 'As long as we are together, nothing else matters.'

He nodded, then carefully disentangled himself from her arms, fighting to regain control. 'We will be all right,' he repeated. 'But please, do not try to help me again. Things are fine as they are.'

'I will try,' she said with a sigh. But, when he looked into her eyes, there was a spark of unquenched rebellion waiting for the moment she forgot her promise and tried again.

He loved her.

He had not said it in so many words, but she could feel it in the way he held her. Even he had to admit that things were better, now that they had each other. But the feeling raised almost as many questions as it answered.

If he loved her, why had he insisted he did not? Or, as Edward had said, was she just confused as to what it meant to be in love? And did he feel the same for his mistress as he felt for her? Worse yet, was the feeling stronger?

And what was she to do about Hugh's desire to leave things as they were? He must know that it would be impossible to do as he wished. If she had not meddled, they would not be married, and he would still be sitting alone with a brandy bottle in his father's study.

She nodded in approval as a pair of footmen hung the last panel of the drapes at the study window. The afternoon sun streamed into the room, bringing out the colours on the Aubusson rug she had chosen.

She took a deep breath and smiled. Even the air felt better, like lemon and beeswax from the freshly polished bookshelves that would be behind the new desk. She ran her hand lightly along the neat row of journals bound in red leather, the date of each year embossed in gold on the spine.

Then she paused. There was a book for 1812 and another for 1814. The current year had been sitting on the surface of the desk. But 1813, the year of the old duke's death, was missing.

'Your Grace,' the butler called from the hall. 'Are you ready for the new furniture?' Two more servants were grunting under the weight of the mahogany desk chosen to replace the old one.

'In a moment.' She took note of the papers on the surface then stacked them carefully on a library table on the other side of the room. Then, she turned her attention to the drawers, pulling them out and stacking them beside the papers, so she might transfer the contents. The first three opened easily but the last one resisted.

Then she noted the little brass lock, which was

barely protection at all if Hugh meant to keep the contents secure. She pulled a hairpin from a curl and went to work. The drawer yielded easily and she pulled it out, ready to put it with the others.

Then she looked down. The missing journal sat on top a stack of papers. She stared down at it for a moment, trying to resist. Then she scooped it up, dropped it into her pocket and went back to the re-arranging of the room.

When he returned home for the day, Hugh went to his study and paused at the door in amazement. In the few hours he had been gone, the room had been transformed from the familiar into a place he did not recognise.

The draperies, the carpets and the furniture were all new. He knew the chair by the fire as a mate to the one he found most comfortable when in the salon. The new paper on the walls was his favourite shade of green.

How had she known? They must have discussed personal preferences at some point in the past during the times when they had shared everything with each other. It embarrassed him that he could not recall what she had said to him on those occasions, for it was clear that she had memorised his words for exactly this moment.

As he entered the room, he felt immediately at ease. He could hear the sound of birdsong from the garden outside, no longer deadened by the hangings on the window. The rug under his feet was soft and clean. The stuffy hunt paintings on the wall had been replaced with scenes of the places he had visited on his grand tour. This room was so obviously for him that he did not want to leave it.

'Have the renovations been completed on Her Grace's bedroom?' he asked a passing footman.

The boy shook his head. 'She wanted this done first, and quickly, so that it did not disturb your work.'

'I see,' Hugh said softly. If she had wanted his life to be undisturbed, she might have done nothing at all. But he had to admit, now that he saw the finished project, she had been right to try and change his life. He had not noticed how the sight of the study had depressed him until she had removed the problem.

As she often did, she was putting his needs before her own. He smiled. It might have been nice if she had allowed him to voice his own desires, or even decide what they were by himself. But he had to admit, she had chosen well.

He stepped further into the room and ran a hand over the highly polished wood of the new desk. The papers that he had left on the surface of the old desk had been replaced in approximately the same place on the new one. Alongside them rested a key ring with the small brass key that would unlock the drawers of the desk.

He fitted it into the lock and opened it, surprised

to find the contents of his old desk had been transferred to the new.

Almost all the contents, at least.

He ran a quick hand through the papers, searching for the red leather journal that should be in the left-hand side, but finding nothing.

'Rachel!' He rose and went to the open doorway, searching both ways down the hall. She stepped out of the salon, slowly walking towards him, the journal in her hand and a shocked look on her face.

'Hugh?' She held the book out to him, as if asking for explanation.

'How did you get that?' he demanded.

'I opened the drawer,' she admitted. 'But I did not think…'

'That I would mind your rifling through my personal things?' he finished for her.

'I did not intend to read it. But it is the journal for the time we were together. And I could not resist seeing what you had said.'

'That is also the year my father died,' he reminded her. 'You looked at that, didn't you?'

'There was nothing to see,' she said hurriedly, proving that she had indeed looked.

'After I wrote the story, I tore the pages out and burned them,' he said with a shudder. 'I did not want anyone to see what I had written there.'

'This makes you look guilty,' she said, holding the book out to him. For the first time since they had reunited, her face was full of doubt.

'And that is why I kept it locked in a desk drawer,' he replied with a laugh. 'I did not intend for it to be read by you or anyone else.'

'I cannot un-see what I have read,' she said. 'But you can explain it to me.' She came into the study and dropped the book on the desk. 'Your secret is safe with me, whatever it is.'

'Even if I have done something unspeakable?' he asked, watching her closely.

'I am your wife,' she said, holding out her hands to him. 'I can help you, if you let me.'

He looked around the room, searching for a way to avoid the conversation that he knew was coming. But it wasn't the same room, the one that had held his secrets for so long. It was as if she had reached into his heart to create a safe place where he could be the man he was meant to be.

He could refuse to speak of it. But, until she had read the journal, her faith in his innocence was the one true constant in his life. If he did not tell her the truth, her imagination might create something even worse than what he had actually done.

Now she followed him into the room and shut the door behind them, leaning against the panels as if she feared he could grab her and put her out.

'Tell me the truth,' she said. Then she waited.

Chapter Seventeen

She never should have opened the drawer, much less read what she had discovered there. Now, instead of enjoying the redecorated study, Hugh seemed to have aged ten years.

'You think you understand what happened here the night my father died. But you only do to a point. Much happened after you were gone and I made sure that the people who knew of it could never speak a word of it. Are you really sure you want to share the knowledge?'

'I was here that night and it changed my life, as it changed yours,' Rachel said, staring into his tired green eyes. 'I want to know the real reason that you rejected me and are rejecting me still. If our vows in the church mean anything at all to you, know that I own a share of whatever it is you are hiding. Give it to me.'

He gave her an anguished look, as if this burden was the last thing he wished to give her. Then, he began. 'The night of the murder—before I met with you—I argued with my father at dinner over money.'

'Everyone knows that,' she said with a dismissive wave of her hand. 'The servants spread the tale almost immediately.'

'But no one mentioned that it was not the least bit uncommon. As a family, we argued often and over everything. Sometimes I thought that the old man enjoyed seeing us at each other's throats. My sisters wanted money as much as I did and that night they were arguing over a dress. Peg had been wearing Olivia's gowns about the house and angling for a season. There was one gown, a green net, that was in particular contention. Olivia claimed that Peg had ruined it.'

'What does any of this have to do with your father's death?' she asked.

'The night it happened, as I was going up the stairs to wait for you, I saw one of my sisters in a green dress going into my father's study.'

'Which one?'

'I am not sure,' he said with a shrug. 'Father refused to spend money on candles if it was only family in the house and did not keep the halls lit. That night I did not see much more than a flash of blonde hair and a swish of that green skirt before the door closed.' He gave her a sad smile. 'Since we were up to no good, I did not want to see her any more than I wanted her to see me.'

Rachel had not thought of it at the time, but the

house had always been uncommonly dark when she'd visited it. All the same, there was nothing about what he was claiming that seemed worthy of melodrama. 'So you saw one of your sisters going to wish your father goodnight,' she said with a shrug. 'There is nothing so mysterious about that.'

'When I was called downstairs to see the body, there was a green spangle in the blood on the desk. No one noticed but me. I hid it.'

Rachel laughed, for she could not help herself. 'You are not accusing your sisters of the crime of murder?' It had to be a coincidence, or a mistake. Nothing more than that.

'I did not want to,' he said. 'It was Olivia who found the body and she was wearing a blue dress when she did so. It was different from the one she had worn at dinner. And Margaret was wearing her nightgown when I saw her next. Neither one wore green.'

'I can see why you did not tell the Runners such a tale,' she said. 'It would have seemed more dishonourable for you to accuse your sisters.'

He gave her an exasperated look. 'People have been hanged on less information than that. I had my suspicions, but the Runners wanted it to be me. They could not prosecute without evidence, so I held my tongue and let them believe what they liked.'

'And is that all?' she asked, unimpressed.

'If that had been all, I'd have chosen to forget, assumed it a trick or a mistake. But the next day a maid came to me with a scrap of the gown, stained with blood and charred from burning. She said she found it in the fireplace of an unused guest room.'

Rachel frowned. There was likely an explanation for it, but she could not think what it would be. 'Did you go to your sisters to ask about it?'

'Later, after things had settled, I asked them both. Olivia claimed to have given it to Margaret, and Peg said she did not know what had happened to it.'

'Strange for a dress that they liked well enough to fight over,' she admitted.

'I wish that were all,' he said, shaking his head as if he did not want to continue. 'The next night, the maid that came to me with the dress was found dead on the lawn. Strangled with Peg's hair ribbon.'

'I heard nothing about this!' Rachel said, shocked.

'Because I saw to it that you did not,' he replied, sinking into a chair and burying his face in his hands. 'I did not call the Runners. I made the footman who had found her get a cart from the stables. Then I drove to the Thames and dumped the body.' He shook his head again and reached for the brandy bottle that sat on the side table, pouring a glass for Rachel as well.

She took it and drank, letting the liquor burn its way down her throat, and gasping for air.

'And that is the sort of man you have married,' he said with a bitter laugh. 'One that treated a family servant as if she had no value at all.'

'The poor girl,' she whispered. 'Did no one ask after her?'

'The butler assured me that she had no family. Even so, the poor thing deserved more than I gave her. I pensioned the butler and sent the footman that helped us home to his family with references and a heavy purse. And then I set to keeping my sisters out of society so that what happened to their maid would not happen to anyone else.'

'You punished both of them?' she asked, shocked.

'What else could I do? The evidence conflicts. And I have searched for years for a clue that did not point to them. Everyone in the house can be accounted for. One of them did this, which means one of them is surely mad. And if one is mad, then perhaps both are.' He was shaking his head again. 'Perhaps I am as well. I can assure you, I am not as sane as I was when I began this and madness often runs in families.'

'But surely, since nothing has happened in two years…?'

He laughed. 'Less than one year. Despite my efforts to contain them, Olivia has been meeting men in secret. Her suitor Richard Sterling was found in the river with a knife in his back.'

'It could have been a coincidence,' Rachel suggested, not really believing her own words.

'Coincidences happen too often in this family,' Hugh said with a bitter smile. 'The *ton* has no problem believing that I was the one that killed him. And

I have no trouble believing it was one of my sisters. Probably Liv.' He paused. 'I cannot manage to believe Peg capable. But that is because I am too soft, not because she could not manage it, if she thought she was protecting her sister...'

'And now they are both married,' Rachel said.

'And Liv's husband has been attacked on the street,' Hugh added, taking a drink. 'The man might as well have dug his own grave by marrying into this family. And you...' He reached out to take her hand. 'If I have put you at risk...'

'What reason would anyone have for hurting me?' Rachel asked, then took another sip of the brandy and tried not to think of one.

'What reason would they have to leave you safe? What reason has there been for any of this?' Hugh asked with a shrug. 'That is why I fear madness. Sane people do not solve their problems with wholesale butchery. Their actions cannot be predicted.'

'And you have been taking the blame all this time?'

'Because nothing could be done to me,' he said in a tone that made it all sound very logical. 'The protection of the peerage does not extend to my sisters. And I have seen the sort of places that they could be remanded to, should charges be brought. Horrible prisons, and hospitals and asylums nearly as bad. And then there is the hangman's noose. I don't know if my influence could save them.'

'Surely it would not come to that?' she asked, not wanting to believe.

'I do not know how else it will end,' he said. 'And now they are both out of my house and I have no control over them at all. I have but to wait for their husbands to discover what sort of family they have married into. Solomon has already been here, complaining of attacks on his life. It is not over,' he said with another shake of his head.

'You did your best,' she assured him.

'And it was not good enough. Now that I have lost control, it is beginning again.'

'And there is no reason to believe that it is a family problem. You are not affected,' she said, still not wanting to believe.

'And there is no way to prove that it is not,' he said. 'I do not think I am likely to run mad and kill as my sisters might, but I am prone to nightmares, black moods—melancholy and hopelessness that never seems to lift. I did not want to risk your future by intertwining it with mine but, now that it has been done, I refuse to bring a child into the world only to have it suffer as I am suffering.'

It did not make his rejection of her any easier, but it at least made sense.

'You understand what this means for us,' he said. 'It is why I do not want to take the risk of lying with you. Whatever this is, it must end with my generation.'

'I understand,' she said, still not sure that she did. 'But that does not mean that we cannot be friends.'

'Friends?' he said, as if the word was alien to him.

'I am not afraid of you. I never was,' she reminded him. 'I understand you better than anyone else in the world. And we are married, after all. I should think that makes us friends.'

He laughed. 'You make it sound easy. It is not. At least, not for me. My past friendship with you led to nothing but trouble.'

'Surely it was not that bad?' she asked, biting her lip to fight back the sob forming in her throat. If he could speak thus of their past, she wondered if she had truly understood anything that had happened between them.

'I took advantage of your innocence and you wasted your future because of it. Now you have roped yourself to me and there is nothing I can offer that will give you the future you deserved to have. That is why I would prefer it if distance is kept between us. Anything more will make our lives more complicated than they need to be.'

'It is almost the end of the season,' she reminded him. 'Perhaps it will be easier when we are out of London.'

'We?' he said, his eyes darkening.

'In the past, you have retired to the country at the end of the season,' she reminded him. 'Except for last year, when you remained...' She blushed, for the statement made it clear how closely she had been watching him during their separation, mooning after him from a few yards away.

'Because of my sisters' needs,' Hugh said. 'I thought it best to stay here.' Then he cleared his throat. 'This year, there is no reason you cannot go to Suffolk. I suspect there are many improvements you will need to make on the house. It has been some time since there has been a lady in residence. Not since my mother was alive, and she died at Margaret's birth.'

'Are you sending me away?' Rachel demanded, shock in her voice.

'Not away,' he muttered. 'The estate is mine, after all. You like riding. The gardens are very fine, and larger than the one we have here. You will be very happy there.'

'I did not marry you for your property,' she said, unable to hide the hurt from her voice.

'And I did not marry you to listen to you argue,' he said, then changed his tone. 'It will be easier for both of us if we are not together.'

'Because you are afraid that your children will be mad,' she said.

'Because I am afraid,' he agreed, unashamed to admit it. 'Now that I cannot watch out for my sisters, I had hoped for a small degree of peace in my life, and I will not find it sharing a house with you.'

'I see,' she lied, then added, 'But the season is not over just yet. We will have two weeks together at least. I am sure we can learn to make the best of it.'

He smiled back at her, clearly relieved that she was agreeing after only a small amount of argument. 'I think we can both control ourselves, now that I have explained what is at risk.' Then, before she could make an objection, he held out a hand for the journal she had been holding. When she offered it to him, he locked it in the drawer of his new desk, then sat down and contentedly began shuffling his papers as if all the problems they had discussed were settled.

Without another word, she left the room. She had much to think about and even more to do.

After her departure, Hugh leaned back in his chair, suddenly weak. Perhaps it was the wound from the duel that was still bothering him, or perhaps it was simply the conversation they'd had and the weight that had been lifted from his spirit.

Someone knew.

She had always known part of it, of course. But her conviction of his innocence had been more of a problem than a relief. What was the good of having an alibi when one did not dare use it? The assumed truth of what had happened here had clung to him like mud. But the reality was worse and he had not wanted to expose her to it.

But now? He had told her everything, and she had not left him. He could not manage to express the feeling of waking each day, for years, and fearing that there would be another death to cover. Or the dreams that plagued him of the feel of cold, dead flesh and the final splash as a body slid into the river.

How could she understand or forgive a thing that he could not forgive himself?

But she had listened, and she had not run.

It was as if he had been bound so long that he had lost all feeling. And, suddenly, someone had cut one of the ropes. Sensation was flooding back into his dormant spirit.

And it ached.

The sudden return of feeling made some hurts even more acute. What was he to do with a wife that he wanted but could not have? Would it ever be possible to speak freely to her whenever he wanted and have her listen, as she had today? Of all the things he missed about the old times, he'd forgotten how much he liked talking with her.

He had been so intent on the journal and its contents that he had forgotten to thank her for what she had done in the study. When he looked around him, the space was as comforting as a hug. Now that the book was locked away again, it was as if the problem was contained and he was free of it.

And, though it was bittersweet, in a week or two he would be free of the continuous temptation that was Rachel. His life would be lonely but safe. He could not hope for much more than that.

Chapter Eighteen

Rachel stood in the doorway of the Duchess's suite, staring in approval at the servants hanging paper and taking down the old draperies. She had done much good since coming here and would do even more, given the chance. But she could do nothing for Hugh if he carried out his plan to cart her off to the country like so much unwanted furniture.

Two years ago, when she had convinced him to allow her into his rooms, she had been impulsive to the point of foolishness, but they had never been discovered. When she had tricked him into marriage, he had been angry. But, with time, she was proving that he had no reason to hate her. Even if he was no longer willing to love her, they were just as well suited as they'd ever been.

Today, she had shown a similar lack of foresight when she had gone through his desk drawers. But it had come out right again and precipitated a revelation that Hugh had managed to keep hidden from everyone else.

She could not deny that her impulses sometimes led her to wild and unladylike activities. But she meant no harm, and it seemed that her instincts were good. Everything worked out for the best.

Which led to the question of what she should do now. She could allow Hugh to proceed with his plan and abandon her in Suffolk, alone and unloved. And he would be here, lonely and in the same city as the exotic beauty from Vauxhall Gardens.

It was probably unworthy of her to be so jealous. But she had seen the way that woman had looked at Hugh, like a hungry lioness staring at a meal. It would be extremely unwise to leave him alone with her.

She glanced out of the window into the peace of the garden and was surprised to see Mr Clement sitting on the bench under the oak tree. He seemed to notice her and raised a hand in welcome, beckoning her to come down and speak.

She hurried down the back stairs and out through the kitchen door to find him still waiting, a smug smile on his face, as if he felt he belonged there. He gestured to the empty dog house. 'I must say, this space is much nicer now that Olivia's dogs are gone from it. I miss her quite horribly, but it would be a lie to say I miss those dogs.'

'You really are not allowed here, you know,' Rachel said with a worried shake of her head and a glance at the study where Hugh might be.

Clement sighed. 'I have treated the space as my own for so long it is difficult to let it go. Olivia and I met here, you see.'

She nodded, thinking of her visits to Hugh, and wondering if his sister had had the nerve for such intimacies under an open sky where anyone might have seen them. She suspected not. But that did not make her time with Clement any less precious. 'But, in the end, she did not choose you?' The question was part commiseration and part a reminder that what this man had shared in was over.

'Solomon came along,' Clement said with a frown and a shake of his head. 'He was here and everything changed.'

'And Olivia...' Rachel said, thinking of all Hugh suspected about her. 'Were her affections for you not true?'

'They seemed so,' he said, shaking his head. 'I do not know what Solomon could offer that I could not. But he came and everything between us changed.'

He might not know but, having seen Mr Solomon, Rachel was able to speculate. While Mr Clement might claim to be miserable at the loss of Olivia, it was Mr Solomon she pictured when she thought of one suffering from a broken heart.

But today, she gave Mr Clement's hand a pat and tried encouragement. 'I am sure you are sad for now. But there will be other women, and other loves.'

'Not for me,' he said firmly. 'Never for me.' His jaw was set and his expression cool. He looked as Edward had when he'd insisted on the need for a duel, as if his will had been thwarted and he had no real interest in the reason that the woman he'd chosen had not chosen him.

'Well, Olivia no longer lives here,' Rachel reminded him as gently as she could, wishing he would go away and take his bitterness with him.

'Are you aware of her new direction?' he asked, staring at her expectantly.

It was in the house in her writing desk. But what would it do for the poor fellow other than give him an excuse to haunt someone else's garden? A white lie would be a mercy. She shook her head. 'Hugh and his sisters are estranged, and he would prefer that I not try to heal the breach.'

'That is most unfair of him,' he said.

'He is the master of the house and there is little I can do without his permission.' Another lie. But she much preferred that he think it was Hugh's idea to keep him away from Olivia and not her own.

Clement reached into his pocket and offered her another of his cards. 'If you discover her location, please contact me. If only so that I may see her one more time.'

'Of course,' she agreed weakly, trying not to shiver as he excused himself and exited through the gate, latching it behind him as if it were his own property.

* * *

That night was the night of the long-awaited Folbroke ball, her first official appearance as the Duchess of Scofield. She dressed with the same care she
had on her wedding night, donning the gown that her
modiste had guaranteed was designed to set tongues
wagging. It was blue silk a shade deeper than her
eyes, with skirts sprinkled with diamante stars and
a bodice cut lower than anything she had worn in
public before.

She looked in the mirror and smiled. It was not
the *ton* she meant to attract with this daring ensem-
ble. If Hugh did not notice her tonight, he was as
dead as his father.

There was a knock on the door and her maid appeared, arms laden with several jewel cases. 'His
Grace said they are yours if you wish them and to
take what suits you.'

'Thank you,' Rachel said, trying not to frown. She
had imagined Hugh draping her neck with sapphires,
his touch hot on the skin of her throat and his breath
tickling her ear as he whispered his appreciation of
her looks. But apparently he could not be bothered
and she was to do it herself.

She refused to let the maid see her displeasure.
'Let us see what he has sent.'

She rejected emeralds as the wrong colour, and
the pearls as too common. But the third box held
a rather simple necklace of silver chains adorned
with a single diamond drop that rested in her cleav-

age and drew attention to her breasts. After Rachel put it on, they dressed her hair with matching silver combs and diamond pins.

Her look complete, she stepped back from the dressing table to admire herself. She looked older than she had just a day ago, sophisticated and knowing, very like a married woman and not the scared virgin that she was. Most importantly, she looked how she imagined a duchess should look.

If she could do nothing else for Hugh, she could make him proud when they were in public together and be the sort of woman he deserved to have married—one who was gracious and beautiful and who held her head high above the rumours that people wanted to spread. There would be talk, of course. There always was when Scofield went out in public. But perhaps this time people would find something good to say about him.

Her preparations finished, she went downstairs to wait for her husband, praying that he had not changed his mind about the whole affair.

As his valet put the finishing touches on his evening clothes, Hugh tried not to think about the night ahead. The outing was likely to be a disaster, but there was nothing to be done about it but force his way through.

He was used to the censure of society and could take it or leave it alone, as he needed. But it had never been his intention to put Rachel through the gossip and snide comments that had become a matter of course for his appearances in public. Knowing what it would be like for her had been one more reason to avoid any chance at a relationship between them.

Her trips to Bond Street and the theatre had given her a taste of what was to come. Unfortunately, the only way to teach her was to let her experience the full derision of the *ton* when attending a ball. Somehow, when one had dressed in one's finest and was feeling well, the whispers hurt more than the idle murmuring that happened at other times.

He let his valet place an emerald stick pin in his lapel and then trotted down the stairs towards doom.

He was halfway to the ground floor before he noticed the vision awaiting him in the hall. The blue silk clung to her body, barely covering her soft white breasts. Diamonds sparkled in her black hair like stars in a night sky. And suddenly he was two years younger and seeing her with all the carefree hunger he used to. His heart was in his throat; it was impossible to speak.

Apparently, she had no such trouble. 'I did not think I'd be ready before you,' she said, staring up at him where he was frozen in place on the stairs. 'I was afraid you'd changed your mind.'

'No,' he said, and slowly continued his descent, trying to appear as if he was in control of his own life and not ready to offer it to her. 'I gave my word.'

'Of course,' she said, as if just realising the significance of his promise.

'We do not have to go, if you have changed *your* mind,' he assured her. 'We can stay in.'

She laughed at the idea. 'With you in the study and me alone in my finest gown? No thank you. I have had enough of that.'

That was not what he'd imagined at all when he'd suggested it. Instead, he could picture himself, his head in her lap, telling her how he had missed her as she stroked his hair. Then they would go upstairs to his bedroom and he would show her all the things he had promised so long ago.

But then he remembered that there could be none of that, regardless of whether they stayed in or went out. Either way, he was trying to keep his distance, if only to preserve what was left of his sanity.

'We are going out, are we not?' she said. His silence was clearly making her suspicious.

'Of course,' he replied, signalling the footman to summon the carriage, leading her out of the open door and handing her up into her seat. They rode in silence to the ball, and he hid in the shadows on his side, still amazed to find himself married to this goddess.

She had tricked him into it, of course. But tonight he had to force himself to remember that he had ever been angry. Would it really be so bad to succumb to her charms? They could not have children, but perhaps they could come to some understanding. At dinner before the theatre, she had been curious about the pleasures of the flesh that had had nothing to do with procreation. If he could remember to withdraw, they could enjoy all of them. But, if he did not want to embarrass himself in public, if was not something he should be thinking about now.

They arrived at the Folbroke townhouse and Hugh took Rachel's arm, escorting her in and listening to the audible gasp as the footman announced the Duke and Duchess of Scofield. Hugh felt no flinch from the woman at his side, to her credit, and when he glanced down at her, her expression was as serene as if she had walked at his side for a lifetime and not less than a month.

The hostess took her hands as they reached the receiving line and announced her eagerness to meet the new Duchess, and without thinking Hugh searched her face for traces of sarcasm, but it seemed that the countess was sincere. As was her husband, who greeted him with a smile.

Then they passed through the receiving line and came out on the floor surrounded by the other guests. Rachel dropped his arm and readied herself to disappear into the crowd.

'You are leaving me,' he said, surprised.

'We are married now,' Rachel reminded him. 'We can enjoy each other's company any time we wish.' There was a slight and awkward pause after the suggestion, to remind him that the amount he had wished of her company was minimal to non-existent. Then she added, 'And I was under the impression that you had business to attend to that did not concern me.'

'But I thought…' What had he thought? That she would need his protection? She did not seem to think so. He could not claim that he wished to fill her dance card, since he had only grudgingly promised her a single waltz. But suddenly the display of marital *ennui* that he had intended seemed contrived and unnecessary.

'The gossip around me can be vicious,' he said at last.

'But we know it is unfounded, and I will pay it no mind,' she said with a superior look worthy of the wife of a peer.

He smiled back at her, reaching for her hand and raising the gloved knuckles to his lips. He allowed himself to linger over her hand a moment, savouring the warmth of it against his cheek before releasing it, and saying, 'If you need me, I shall be close by.'

'Do not forget that you have promised me the waltz,' she said, holding out her dance card for him to sign. 'Do not think you can escape to the smoking room for the whole night.'

They parted then, or at least attempted to, as he found himself unable to leave, standing in a corner of the ballroom, watching as his wife moved easily from group to group, equally as polite to those who approved and those who did not.

Beside him, he heard a laugh. It was Belston, a fellow peer who, while not exactly a friend, showed no sign that he noticed the cloud that hung over the Scofield title. 'I never thought I would see the notorious Duke of Scofield besotted by a woman.'

'I am not besotted,' Hugh snapped, refusing to take his eyes off Rachel.

'And over his own wife, no less,' the other Duke said with a snigger. 'I know the pain of it. I am so afflicted myself.'

'I have no idea what you are talking about,' Hugh muttered.

'Of course not,' Belston said, still grinning. 'But I fear your intimidating reputation is a thing of the past. After tonight, the *ton* will keep whispering about Scofield, of course. But who can think totally ill of a man with such a charming wife?'

'Thank you,' Hugh said absently, still not sure that what had been said was a compliment. Was that really all it took to change the tide of public opinion? Rachel was as charming and as beautiful as he could wish in a duchess. When he had married her, he had never thought she might be useful, for he had not imagined that she would be seen in public any more than his sisters had been.

But he had kept his sisters in isolation for an entirely different purpose. There was no reason that he could not go about with Rachel all he wished... other than the fact that the nearness of her frightened him in a way it never used to. The last two years of his life had been about rigid control of himself and of others, but suddenly he had joined his life to a woman so uncontrollable that he never knew what she might do next. He could not decide whether to be angry or delightfully surprised.

For the first time in memory, the dangerous Duke of Scofield smiled.

All things considered, Rachel had to admit that it was better being a duchess than it had been when she'd been plain Lady Rachel. There were the usual whispers of scandal, because of her husband, but she was also in the awkward position of being a person so august that the majority of the women—the ones who had not bothered to meet her when she'd been a lesser member of the peerage—were now afraid to speak to her without an introduction.

Fortunately, her hostess was a charming and pleasant woman who seemed more amused by the rumours than anxious to spread them, and she made sure that the other guests were presented to her, parading them past Rachel as if she were a bear in the Tower of London.

In response, Rachel made sure she was equally charming and pleasant, and not at all the sort of woman one would expect to marry a murderer. Between Lady Folbroke's support and her own positive attitude, the women, who had probably planned to shun her, were not quite sure how to go about it.

But she did notice that her dance card remained empty other than the single scrawl of 'Scofield' next to the waltz. Though the other ladies had declared it safe to speak to her, gentlemen, both single and married, gave her a wide birth, unwilling to do anything that might attract negative attention from her husband.

When the waltz started, Hugh reappeared, dutifully ready to dance her around the room. And, as he did, she understood the reason for the boycott.

'You are scowling,' she said, trying not to laugh.

'I beg your pardon?' he queried, turning his attention back to her and away from the single men ringing the floor.

She tapped his shoulder with her fan. 'You look like a dog guarding a bone. Surely you must realise that I am not going anywhere and do not need protecting?'

His expression gentled and he relaxed into the rhythm of the dance. 'I am simply concerned that you will not be received as you should.'

'Of course,' she said, rolling her eyes.

'We can go home whenever you are ready,' he said, but he looked concerned rather than angry for a change.

'Then I may force you to stay until dawn,' she said with a laugh. 'I am having a delightful time.'

He frowned at her in confusion.

'Would you prefer that I be miserable?' she asked.

'Of course not,' he said quickly.

'Because you seem to view outings such as these as a form of punishment.'

'It is probably foolish of me to be so difficult,' Hugh admitted, sounding almost contrite.

'Probably,' Rachel agreed. 'Have you forgiven me for wanting to accept this invitation? Despite your fears, the company has been most diverting.'

'There is nothing to forgive,' he assured her. 'I simply did not want you to be as unhappy as I was.'

'As you were?' she asked, staring up into his eyes. 'And am I to take that as a sign that you are happier now?'

Would it be a mistake to admit that she was right? It had been so long since he had been happy that he was not sure he recognised the feeling. Finally, he cleared his throat and said, 'Recently, there is much that has changed around me. And you are the cause of it.'

'Because you are no longer alone,' she said.

'But I am afraid that you will be,' he replied, giving her hand a light squeeze.

'Not as long as I have you.' She smiled and returned the gesture. 'Now, give me another dance. I do not want to sit down until the sun rises.'

Rachel came close to getting her wish. When they staggered back to the carriage after more dances than she could count, there was a rosy glow in the sky that grew brighter as they drove towards home. She sat on the seat opposite him, unable to help the smile on her face, and unwilling to curb the wicked thoughts flitting through her mind.

He must have shared some of them, for he was smiling as well, and shaking his head in warning.

'Did you have a good evening?' she asked, smug.

'Better than I've had in a very long time,' Hugh admitted.

'Because of me,' she said with a proud nod.

'You may have had something to do with it,' he replied.

'Perhaps, next season, we can throw a ball of our own.'

'No one will come,' he said quickly, but his smile did not fade.

'Then it will be just the two of us, drinking all the champagne and dancing all the dances.'

'I cannot imagine a better evening,' he said with a sigh. Then the carriage drew to a stop at their front door and he helped her down...

And went through the front door without her.

She gave her skirts a frustrated swish and hurried after him, but he paid her no mind, continuing up the stairs to his room and blowing her a kiss before shutting the door against her.

She continued on to the next door, her freshly remodelled room. The silk on the walls was her favourite shade of blue, as were the curtains on the bed and the windows. But none of it brought her any happiness because she was still alone. There was one way that a night like this should end and it was not lying alone in one's bed, scant yards from the man who could change everything.

Without bothering to call her maid, she slipped out of her gown, shift and stockings, letting down her hair one pin at a time until the curls tickled her bare shoulders. The diamond necklace remained, swaying in invitation between her breasts. She stared at it in the mirror, fascinated.

Then, she pulled on the nightgown that she had chosen for her wedding night and covered it with a silk wrapper before walking across the room and opening the connecting door that led to her husband's room.

She glanced into the room on the other side of the threshold to see Hugh, bare chested, sitting on his bed and pulling off his boots. He froze, staring at her, then he gathered his dignity and said, 'Is there something that I can help you with?'

She smiled. 'No. I was just…' She stepped back from the door. 'I find the room rather close tonight and thought an open door might help.' It was a transparent lie and she waited to hear him suggest an open window, or even unlatching the hall door.

Instead, he continued to stare.

She unbelted the wrapper she was wearing and let it fall to the floor. 'That is somewhat better.'

His boot dropped to the floor with a thump.

She turned and walked back towards her bed, letting her hips sway in invitation. Then she reached to her throat and undid the top buttons on her nightdress. She stretched, feeling the bodice slip on her shoulder and her skin chill at the exposure to the night air.

There was the thump of a second boot.

Her breath caught in her throat.

'Rachel.'

She had grown used to the tone he used when calling her name, and the faint upward inflection to indicate that she had done something to displease him. But this time his voice was softer, and held a warning note, as if there was danger in front of both of them.

'Close the door.'

She undid another button then turned and walked slowly back towards his room. 'This door?' Rachel braced her spine against the door frame and stretched for the door handle to widen the gap at the front of her gown.

He had seen her breasts before—in their hurried grappling in his room two years ago—but never decorated in diamonds when all the night and the rest of their lives lay before them. If only one of them could find the courage to act.

He sighed at the sight of her, breathing slow and deep, as if trying to regain control.

She took a breath of her own and undid the last button. She shrugged out of her nightdress, letting it fall to the floor as the robe had done. Then she stood before him, naked for the first time, stepped away from the door into his room and closed it behind her, exactly the opposite of what he had asked for.

'Rachel,' Hugh said again with amused resignation.

'It was a lovely night, wasn't it?' Rachel tempted.

'Not as lovely as you,' he admitted.

'I don't want for it to end,' she said, staring into his eyes.

'I told you before...' he warned with a sigh.

'That you did not love me,' she said, then forced herself to smile and continued. 'But you do want me. And, for tonight, that is enough.'

She walked towards the bed, trying not to shiver as her nipples tightened from the cold air against her bare skin. When she reached the bed, she sat beside him, so close that her arm brushed his and warmth flooded into her again.

He touched her cheek, stroking a thumb along her jawline. 'You don't know what you are playing with. It is known all over London that I am a very dangerous man.'

Rachel laughed. 'Not to me,' she said, turning her head to bite the pad of his thumb.

'There is madness in my family,' he reminded her, his voice serious, though he did not withdraw his hand. 'It should not be propagated.'

'Propagated.' She tasted the word. 'You make it sound like we are about to plant tulips.'

'It is not a joking matter,' he said. 'Time has changed me. I am not the same man I was. I was not worthy of your hand then and I am not worthy of your body now.'

'Then how about my lips?' she asked, closing her eyes and tipping her face up to receive his kiss.

There was a pause of only a moment. Then he groaned and she felt his cheek rub against hers, the stubble rough on her skin. He turned his head and their lips met, softly at first, then hungrily, as if it was possible to make up for all the lost time in a single night.

Her tongue found his and they kissed, as he had taught her two years ago—deeply, as if life itself depended on the contact. His hand tightened on her shoulder, a finger hooking in the necklace she still wore and tracing down the length of it to settle against the pendant between her breasts.

She pressed a hand flat against his chest, fingers spread. 'I have dreamed of this moment since you left me,' she whispered. 'Every night, I touch myself and I wish you were beside me.'

He groaned and pulled her body tight to his, pushing her back to lie on the bed. 'I am lost without you. But I cannot trust myself with you. What am I to do?'

'Give in,' she murmured.

He needed no further urging. He struggled out of his breeches and re-joined her on the bed to take her in his arms.

She stole a look down the length of him, both shocked and amazed at so much bare skin. Before, when they had been together in this room, she had revealed far more than she had seen. Now she could admire his broad chest and the fascinating trail of hair that led down his belly, directing her eyes to his erection.

He tipped her face back up to look into his eyes,

which were full of mirth at her curiosity. 'Soon,' he whispered and kissed his way from her lips down her shoulders as his hands stroked her breasts.

She sighed then, leaning into him to enjoy the weight of his hands on her and the gentle flutter of his tongue on her collar bone. She let her hands rove through his hair, cradling his head against her body and urging his lips lower to take her nipple. When he did, the feeling arched through her and left her with no thought beyond the pleasure of the moment.

And then, his mouth continued its journey south, circling her navel before delving into it. Then Rachel remembered something he had promised to do when they used to meet in secret, something that had sounded too wicked to be possible. His mouth was between her legs now, searching, finding, kissing, driving her mad.

She remembered the first time he had brought her to climax with a few easy strokes of his hand and a caution to be still, lest anyone hear them together. She had wondered then if it was exciting because it was forbidden. But this was even better and she needn't be quiet. She could scream in ecstasy if she wanted or come on a whisper.

As if he could sense her dilemma, Hugh laughed against her skin, nipping and licking until she dissolved into uncontrolled moans and gave herself up for him. Then he rose from between her legs and hovered over her for a moment before urging her to spread her legs.

She reached for him, holding him at the waist, guiding him to her. His fingers stroked her now in the place where she was wet and eager, spreading the lips of her sex and murmuring that he did not mean to hurt her.

She closed her eyes, braced herself and felt him slide into her as if they had been formed to join by God. It must have been so, for why else would it feel so good? He was taking her to heaven with slow thrusts of his body, cupping her bottom and urging her to move in harmony with him, equal and opposite.

She could feel the climax approaching like a wave building far out at sea. Her body tightened on his as her nails dug into the flesh of his back and his pace quickened. Then he whispered in a passion-drugged voice, 'I mustn't...'

Unless he meant that he mustn't stop, she did not want to hear it. He had spent far too much time telling her what was wrong and avoiding this moment, something that was clearly right. So she kissed him, hoping that he would forget. He responded, just as she knew he would, as hungry for her as she was for him.

Then, suddenly, he was gone. He broke the kiss, freed himself from her arms and her body, then rolled away and turned his back to her, spending in the sheet with a quick jerk of his hand.

For a moment, he did not move, neither reaching for her nor moving further away. She could hear his breath growing more even as the last of the passion drained from him and his blood cooled. Only then did he reach for her, his hand settling between her legs to try and finish what he had started.

This was what he had meant about control and how he prevented children with his mistress. He had claimed that he could not love her in the same way because he would not be able to control himself.

Apparently, he had lied.

Tonight had proved that he was more than capable of resisting her, even in the throes of passion. He had denied her her due as his wife—the completion of the act. Apparently, when the moment came to decide, he had found she was no different from one of his whores.

She evaded his hand, rolling away and trying to ignore the ache in her body, the longing to be touched and to feel the rush of ecstasy that she knew he could bring her to. She had told him that desire was enough, that love was not needed. But she was wrong.

His hand settled on her hip and his lips grazed her ear. 'Are you sure?' He stroked her side, then settled his hand over her breast. 'We need not be finished, if you are not done. And if the first time did not hurt…'

'It hurt,' she lied. Or was it a lie? She hurt in spirit, if not in body, a pain that she did not know how to explain. To avoid conversation, she curled inwards, hugging her stomach and pulling her knees up to her body.

His hand withdrew, settling on her shoulder. 'I understand. I will give you time. As much time as you need.'

'Thank you,' she whispered.

And then she waited for the words that would salvage the night. If only he would tell her he loved her, she would know that there was hope.

Instead, he kissed the back of her neck and said, 'We have all the time in the world now. I had planned that you would be on your way to Suffolk by the end of the week. But now…'

'Nothing has changed.' She rolled to the edge of the bed and swung her feet to the floor.

'You want to go?' he asked, surprised.

'The season is ending.' She refused to look at him. 'There is no reason to remain in town.'

'I cannot accompany you,' he reminded her. 'Not until I am sure that Solomon is safe from my sister.'

'That is all right,' she said, putting on the false smile she had used for the few women who had snubbed her at the ball. 'Now that we are married, we need not live in each other's pockets. As you have told me before, the manor is just as much your property as this house. It will almost be like being together.' The words were coming too quickly, falling over each other, as if she was trying to convince herself as much as him.

'If that is what you wish,' he said, sounding as confused as she felt.

'That is what I want,' she confirmed, rising now and going towards the connecting door.

'Where are you going?' Now he sounded hurt.

'Back to my room.' She opened the door now and scooped the silk robe off the floor, wrapping her body in it and hiding from his view. 'I have to begin packing tomorrow and need to get some sleep.'

'Of course,' he said. His voice was distant, as if they were separated by miles and not just the length of the room. 'Sleep well, my dear.'

'And you,' she said, shutting the door.

When she had gone, Hugh settled himself into the small, warm spot where her body had been, trying to fix the best of what had just happened in his memory so he might never lose it.

Like so many of the important moments of his life, he had bungled this badly. But this time he was not even sure what he had done. She had been near to orgasm, just as he had been. But by the time he had finished, he had lost her in body, mind and spirit.

He should have known better. But he had expected lying with her to have something in common with previous life experience. He had bedded women before. But he had kissed them as well and, as kisses with Rachel had always been better, it should have been a warning that when the moment came to withdraw he should stay.

But giving himself to her in that way had felt too dangerous, and not just because of the risk of children. It would be like an outpouring of the spirit to come inside her, as if he'd have been giving up his very soul. And, since he was not even sure he had a soul after all that had happened, he certainly did not deserve the divine redemption of the angel he had married.

As it had been her first time, he should have been the generous lover he had promised himself he would be. Instead, it seemed he had hurt her without noticing. He had been selfish, used her for his pleasure then turned from her to finish. In the moments that had taken, he had lost her.

Perhaps it was for the best that she leave. It would be easier on both of them if they did not see each other for a while. She would have more freedom to do as she pleased. And he would have his old life back, such as it was. There would be no great joy, but neither would there be a continual risk of succumbing to passion and producing children as mad as him and as uncontrollable as their mother.

But why did something that sounded rational, right and in control feel completely wrong?

Unable to answer the question, he rolled over to his own side of the bed and tried to sleep.

Chapter Nineteen

The next morning, Rachel considered getting up to ride with Hugh, to prove that she still had her pride. Then she pounded her pillow and rolled over, giving it up as a bad job. It would take more than a fine habit and a dust of powder to make her look other than what she was: a woman who'd had more tears than sleep.

Last night, she had run from him when a more experienced woman might have stayed to fight. She had announced that she would go away, just as he'd wanted, but some part of her had hoped to hear him contradict her. He could have asked her to stay. He might have said he could not live without her.

She was being a fool. She doubted the mystery woman from Vauxhall would have played coy in the same situation. Instead, she'd have said what she wanted, and used her body to see to it that Hugh never let her go.

And she might do it still if Rachel retreated from

London at the first sign of defeat. But what else cou
she do?

She rang for chocolate and toast to be brought
to her room. Then she splashed her face with cold
water and instructed her maid to begin the packing.
If she wanted her marriage to work, she had three
days to persuade her husband that he loved her and
could not live without her. As it had taken two years
to get this far, it seemed an incredibly short amount
of time to bring about a miracle.

And then there was the matter of her investiga-
tion into what had happened on the night Hugh's father had died. But, as the Bow Street Runners had
proved worthless, what was she to do on her own?

The matter was decided when she opened the afternoon post and found a note from Lady Margaret
Castell, announcing that she and her sister would
be visiting tomorrow and were eager to reacquaint
themselves with their new sister-in-law. She must
get them to open their minds as well and prove that
Hugh's suspicions were not correct.

Promptly at ten the next morning, Rachel heard
a knock on the front door and the butler announced
that Lady Olivia and Lady Margaret had been shown
to the green salon. She called for tea to be laid and
went to meet them, suddenly anxious.

It was not bad enough that Hugh had filled her
mind with suspicions about the sanity of his family. When they had played together as children, the

girls had been her social superiors and she had never quite overcome her awe of them. Now she had married Hugh, she was the mistress of their childhood home. How would they receive her when much of society had turned their backs on her for marrying their brother?

When she came into the room, it was hard to think of the two elegant ladies sitting there as having once been her childhood friends, Liv and Peg. Margaret had changed even more since last Rachel had seen her. Judging by the gentle swell of her stomach, she would be a mother in a few more months.

'Welcome,' Rachel said, sitting down and gesturing the servants to serve the tea and cakes. 'It is so good to see you again after all this time.'

'We were rather surprised at your invitation, Your Grace,' Lady Olivia admitted in a formal tone, 'As we are under the impression that our brother has still not forgiven us for eloping.'

'Please, call me Rachel, as you used to,' she began, smiling in what she hoped was an open and friendly way.

'It has been some time since we have talked together,' Margaret said, smiling back at her.

'Two years at least,' Olivia agreed and frowned. 'We can blame Hugh for that.'

'Well, do not worry about Hugh's welcome today,' Rachel assured them. 'I am sure he did not mean to ban you from the house.'

Of course, she had not actually warned him

that they would be coming today. But she was sure enough that he would not mind their presence, should he notice it. 'I am sure he is most concerned for your welfare and happiness,' Rachel said, trying to dispel the worried looks the sisters were giving her. 'He wants the best for you, though I will admit he sometimes does a bad job of showing it.'

Now the girls were passing doubtful looks between them, as if remembering everything he had done to keep them contained, and wondering how any of it could have been for their own good.

Rachel reached for her tea. 'But he is not the only person in the family now. I thought I would make it clear that I hold no animosity towards you and am eager to see any breach there might be between your brother and the pair of you healed.'

'That is most generous of you,' Olivia replied, taking her cup. 'I will admit that I wondered, when we were not invited to the wedding.'

How was she to answer this? Rachel cleared her throat. 'It was a hurried affair. I was rather more concerned that the groom attended than worrying about guests.'

'We read the news of it in the scandal sheets,' Margaret said with a giggle. 'And my husband told me of the duel,' she added in a more sombre tone.

'I was most impressed that Hugh managed to persuade a girl to be alone with him, much less allowed himself to be caught that way,' Olivia finished.

'It was mostly my doing,' Rachel admitted. 'But when one is in love…'

'Love?' Both the girls spoke in shocked unison.

Rachel nodded. 'It is quite hopeless, I am afraid. I have been in love with him since we were girls, though I did not tell you, for fear that you would tease me. There is nothing I can do to change my feelings for him.'

The two stared at each other, still in shock at this revelation, and Lady Olivia admitted, 'We were wondering if, after less than a month with Hugh, you called us here to ask for sanctuary.'

'And how does he feel about you?' Margaret blurted, then looked down into her tea cup, embarrassed.

'He swore he would never marry, you see,' Olivia informed her. 'He is still in love with someone from his past…'

'That is me!' Rachel announced, then blushed as she remembered that he had denied just such that emotion on their wedding night. 'Well, at least… He made promises of marriage before your father died.'

'Then you are…' The two girls looked at her, alarmed, then stared towards the door, as if eager to depart.

Then Margaret seemed to gather her nerve and asked, 'Were you here, in the house, on the night that our father died?'

'I was in your brother's room,' she admitted. 'Hugh did not do it, if that is what you are concerned about. I was with him when the body was discovered. We heard the screams from downstairs.'

'Then you were not the one who screamed first?' Margaret asked, a confused look on her face.

'I do not understand,' Rachel responded.

'Before Olivia got to the study, there was a scream,' she replied. 'We had learned of your presence in the house—though not your identity, of course—and we assumed that it must have been you who screamed.'

'It was not,' she said with a sigh. 'I came straight to your brother's room and did not leave until after the crime was committed. I am his alibi and he is mine.'

There was a moment of confused silence. Then Margaret said, 'You can offer no other information on the identity of the killer?'

Rachel shook her head.

Olivia's expression dropped in disappointment. 'We assumed that, when and if we found you, you would have the answer to the whole thing.'

'I was rather hoping that you could answer questions for me,' she said, trying not to sound threatening. 'The night of the murder, was one of you wearing a green gown?'

'The green net with the spangles,' Olivia said with a sigh. 'I have not thought about that for years.'

'So it was you?' Rachel asked, surprised that the truth would be so easy to find.

'No,' Olivia said. 'By that time, Peg had ruined it and I had given it to her.'

'And I had no idea what happened to it,' Margaret said. 'I assumed the maid stole it when she ran away.'

'Your maid ran away?'

'Right after the murder,' Olivia said. The pair of them were looking at Rachel with large, guileless eyes, and it was clear that they were either the best liars in England or completely innocent of the crime Hugh accused them of, for they had no idea that the maid was dead.

Rachel continued cautiously. 'The night your father was killed, your brother saw a woman wearing a green gown going into the study. He assumed it was one of you.'

'Us?' The girls laughed in unison.

'What utter nonsense,' Olivia added.

'Why did he not simply ask us what we were doing at the time of father's death?' Margaret said.

'I assume it was because he thought you would lie,' Rachel replied. 'And it is true that, unless you can account for each moment of the time between supper and the discovery of the body, we cannot actually prove that you are not guilty.'

At this, the two girls looked at each other for a long, silent moment, then Olivia admitted, 'We have never asked him for the same reason. It was only when we learned of the presence of a mysterious woman in the house that we realised who must have been guilty. But, if it was not you...'

'Then why was he trying to have you committed?' asked Margaret.

Rachel gave a nervous cough. 'I assume, if an asylum was suggested, it was for one or both of you.'

'Us?' Margaret looked thoroughly insulted. 'When I see Hugh next, I will box his ears. The place he considered was quite horrible. I saw it myself.'

'He did not send you there,' Rachel reminded her. 'He kept you in the house instead.'

'We were little better than prisoners here,' Olivia agreed.

'It was because he feared that you would kill again. Your maid did not run away. The body was found in the garden and hidden.'

At this, the two girls sobered. 'Poor Bess,' Margaret whispered.

'And, when Richard Sterling was killed...' Rachel began.

'He thought it was me,' Olivia finished, her face clouding with anger. 'I still have nightmares about that night. And all this time he thought it was me.'

'Since you were equally sure that it was him, it is hardly fair of you to be angry,' her sister replied.

'He treated us horribly,' Olivia reminded her.

'It was not so horrible, really. I suspect father would have been almost as strict. And, if things had been different, we would not have found the husbands we did,' Margaret finished softly.

'While I do not want to minimise how hard this has been on the two of you, I rather hoped that one of you might contribute something that would make matters clearer,' Rachel said, staring from one to the other. 'The culprit is not Hugh, nor was it me. But there were three murders, and someone must have done them. Did you see anything at all that night?'

'I went straight to my room after dinner,' Peg said quickly.

They both turned to look at Olivia.

'And I changed into a darker gown that would not be seen from the windows and met Alister in the garden, as I did every night,' Olivia said, her voice slowing with each word. She was staring at them, staring at her. 'But it could not have been him. I watched him leave and latched the gate behind him.'

'The latch is loose,' Rachel said. 'I have seen him open it myself.'

'And the dog would not have barked because he never barked at Alister,' Margaret added.

Olivia shook her head. 'It could not be him. It simply could not. I have known him for years. What reason could he have had?'

'Father refused him,' her sister reminded her. 'And if the maid saw him in the study and screamed...'

'It could not have been Alister,' Olivia repeated, but this time she began to shake.

'Rachel? What the devil is going on?' Hugh was standing in the doorway, staring at the three of them, especially at the shocked Olivia, who looked near to fainting.

'Alister Clement was in the house that night,' Rachel said, offering no other explanation.

'What do you know of Alister Clement?'

'He has been to visit me in the garden,' Rachel said, surprising everyone. 'He claimed to be a family friend. He was looking for Olivia's direction.'

'Clement,' Hugh said, considering. 'The man didn't have the nerve to elope with Liv. I doubt…'

'He found the nerve once Peg was out of the way,' Liv said, her voice turning bitter. 'He didn't want her to live with us. He didn't want the dogs, either. He just wanted me.' Now she looked sick.

'It would explain Sterling's death,' Hugh said thoughtfully.

'And the maid must have known something,' Rachel finished. 'She was the one to accuse the two of you,' she added.

'If it was Alister, then Liv is still in danger,' Peg said, reaching out for her sister and trying to rub some warmth into her shaking hands.

'As is Solomon,' Hugh said. 'Has he experienced any more attacks?'

'Attacks?' Liv repeated in a whisper. 'What are you talking about?'

'He probably didn't want to worry you,' Hugh said, ringing for a servant. Then he scribbled a quick note at the writing desk in the corner and handed it to the footman when he arrived. 'I am sending for him to come here so that we might get you safely to the country. We will deal with the fellow once we know you will not be hurt.'

'He never meant to hurt me,' Liv said in a strangled voice. 'It is Michael who is in danger.' She stared at her brother with pleading eyes. 'Please do not let him do anything foolish.'

'I will think of something,' Hugh said, then reached in his pocket for a flask and poured a bit of brandy into Olivia's empty cup. 'Drink. It will steady your nerves. And we will need you to be strong for what may lie ahead.'

Chapter Twenty

While they waited for Michael Solomon to arrive, Peg took her sister up to her childhood bedroom, insisting that she lie down for a nap, leaving Hugh alone with his wife.

He turned to her with what was becoming a familiar feeling of exasperation and said, 'You should not have meddled in this.'

'Meddled?' Rachel asked, hands on hips and an equally exasperated expression on her face. 'I may have found an answer to the killings that you could have found long ago if you weren't so set on controlling everything in your reach.'

'I do not…' he insisted. The only thing he had to control right at this moment was his temper.

'You already knew I invited your sisters for tea. It should not have been a surprise to you that they actually decided to come,' she pointed out.

She was right. All the same, it had been a surprise. He'd thought, once they escaped, they would never return here.

'And I talked to them about a matter that concerns us all, just as you could have,' she finished. 'I know your father did not feel that he need listen to anyone else in the family...'

'I am not my father,' he snapped.

'Of course not. But I think sometimes, when you do not know what to do, you behave in a way you think he would approve of.'

'My father was a dictatorial miser,' he said. 'Is that what you think of me?'

'I think you would do well to talk to your sisters,' she said quietly. 'And to trust them, though you were not raised to do so.'

The words stung, though she'd said them gently enough.

'You have no right to lecture me on how I choose to manage my family.'

'Your sisters are grown women and did not need to be managed,' she said, a little more insistently.

'And I suppose next you will be telling me I have no right to decide what is best for you?'

'You have made decisions that affect me because you were afraid of the madness in your family,' she reminded him. 'And now it appears that there is another explanation for what has been happening around you.'

'And until that matter is settled you are going to Suffolk,' he replied, relieved that this, at least, they agreed on. 'And you will be taking Olivia with you. If you are right in your suspicions about Clement, I do not want you anywhere around the man.'

'He did not mean any harm to me when we spoke,' she said.

'And you did not tell me that you have seen him,' he countered, finding his anger again.

'Because I did not think it was important.'

'Because you did not think I would approve, more like,' he replied. 'If that is so, you are right. The man had no right to be trespassing on the property, even if he was not a murderer.'

But what if he was the killer? What if the answer had been right under his nose all along and he had been too proud and too stupid to look for it?

He shook his head to clear it. There would be time enough for recrimination later. Now was the time for action. 'I am not going to let anything happen to you.'

'I am not afraid for myself,' she insisted. 'Clement killed your father. Suppose he decides to kill you as well?'

'He has made no move to do so in two years,' he said with a shrug. 'And, if he is the killer, he does not know that we have discovered the fact. There is no reason to believe that anyone other than Olivia and her husband are at risk. But I will feel better once I know Clement has been caught and has confessed.'

'I have a suggestion,' she said, smiling as she did just before she did something that left him fuming.

He braced himself and gestured for her to continue.

'You should give Alister's card to Mr Pilkington and tell him what we have found. Tomorrow, as planned, we pack my things and send them to Suffolk, along with Olivia, dressed in one of my gowns and wearing a veil. Her husband can accompany her as an outrider, disguised in Scofield livery. You can accompany them as far as needed to be sure they have not been followed.'

'And you?' he asked.

'Will remain in the house so as not to spoil Olivia's disguise.' She smiled. 'If you like, you can put a guard on the house to protect me.'

The plan made a surprising amount of sense. If Solomon agreed, it would be good to see the pair of them safely out of the city before Clement realised they were gone.

'Very well,' he said. 'I will broach the idea with Solomon. In the meantime, continue your packing and explain the plan to Olivia. If they are agreed, we will carry it out tomorrow morning.'

The next day, the carriage was brought round with as much ceremony as possible and loaded with trunks and boxes while Rachel helped Olivia into one of her best day gowns and fixed a thick veil to the brim of the matching bonnet.

Olivia reached out a gloved hand and clasped hers.

'Thank you for this, and for what you have done for Hugh.'

'What have I done for Hugh?'

'You believed in him when no one else did.' Olivia glanced out of the window to where her brother was talking with the coachman. 'He has been very alone all this time.'

'It was his choice to be so,' she said softly, wondering if he would ever change. 'He thinks he can control everything, and that leaves no room in his life for others.'

'I had not thought of him in that way,' Olivia said, surprised.

Rachel thought of how he had been when they'd been in bed together—rigid and disciplined at the moment when they should both have been free. 'You don't know him as I do.' She sighed. 'But let us not think of that now.' There might be a lifetime to contend with that, and she was not sure she could stand it.

So, she focused on completing the transformation of Olivia into a copy of herself. With the veil pinned in place and the disguise complete, she led Olivia through the largely empty house to the front door. The majority of the servants had been dismissed for the day and told that, with the departure of the mistress, there would be no need to lay a hot supper. But in reality it made the departure of the Solomons easier to keep secret.

Then Hugh returned to the house to escort his

sister to the carriage, staring out of the window at the yard. 'The guard that Pilkington has promised is not yet in place.'

'He is probably waiting until the carriage has left so as not to make the departure appear suspicious.'

Hugh nodded but said, 'I do not like it.'

'I will be well,' she said, touching his arm.

'I will follow the carriage until we are free of the city and I am sure that they have not been followed. Then I shall return to you.'

'And we will plan what to do next.' She clasped his hand.

'We most certainly will not,' Hugh replied, pulling away from her. 'You will have no part in what happens next. It is far too dangerous.'

'Mr Clement has no reason to suspect me,' she said.

'And I do not mean to give him one. For once, leave the rest to me.'

She sighed. 'Very well.'

'And, while I am gone, you are to do nothing, you understand? Nothing at all.'

'I am not a fool, Hugh,' she said with a shake of her head.

'I do not think you are,' he said softly. Then he reached for her to kiss her goodbye.

She hesitated for only a moment, then she wrapped her arms around him and kissed him back.

'I will be back tonight,' he whispered, touching her cheek. And then he was gone and she was alone.

She sighed, touching her lips and hoping that she had understood the unspoken message he had left there. If Clement was the killer, there was no reason that they might not have a perfectly ordinary marriage and love each other as husband and wife should. At the very least, he might finally forgive her for the way they had married and admit to his feelings for her.

Or, perhaps what he had given her thus far was all he had to give. If that was the case, she did not know how she could face the future. She had hoped for so much more.

She sighed. Of course, he would have to come back for anything to happen at all. And that return was a few hours from now, at minimum. How was she to spend the time? She went into the library, searching through the books for one that might hold her interest and staring out of the window into the empty garden. There was still no sign of Pilkington's guard, but that man was likely to be an unnecessary precaution, now that Liv and her husband were safely away.

Would it really do any harm if she waited there for him to return? It was not leaving home, after all. But, when she rose to go, she had the strangest sensation as she walked down the hall. It was as if someone was in the house with her.

Then she heard it. A rustling noise was coming from the study. She stepped through the open door to discover Alister Clement rifling the contents of the desk.

He looked up and for a moment their eyes met in silence. Then he drew a gun from his pocket and was across the room before she could think to scream.

'You are supposed to be gone,' he said in a dry, disinterested voice.

'What are you doing here?' she said, backing away until she felt the wall flat against her back.

'The real question is why you are not Olivia,' Clement said with a shrug of impatience. 'She came here with her sister yesterday and did not leave. I had hoped to find her above, in her room.'

'She stayed the night and has gone back to her house,' Rachel replied. 'She was not feeling well after tea.'

'Then who was in the carriage that left for the country this morning?' Clement asked with a raised eyebrow.

'Just my maid,' she said, glancing behind her towards the door.

'In a fine gown and bonnet and with all that luggage?' he said, still sceptical. 'I think it far more likely that you sent Olivia away to keep her safe from me.'

'Why would I do that?' she said, trying to keep her voice calm and slow. 'I thought you were her friend.'

'Because you have discovered the truth,' he said with a sad shake of his head. 'This is most inconvenient. Not at all in line with my plans. And, now that you have seen me, I cannot allow you to tattle.'

'What would I want to tell anyone?' she asked, forcing a smile. But when he looked at her his eyes were devoid of any respect, instead glinting with cold amusement.

'I think we both know the answer to that,' he said. 'You would want to tell that fool of a husband of yours that I killed his father.'

'He already knows,' she said. There was no point in allowing him to think she was alone in the knowledge. 'He knows and he will be back any time now with a man from the Bow Street Runners.'

Clement smiled and applauded, giving a small nod of approval. 'And I am sure you were the one to tell him. No one has suspected me in all this time. It is impressive that you have discovered the truth, but unfortunately the information comes too late to do you any good.'

'I have guessed most of it…' she said, praying that Hugh would come. 'But not all. How did you get past the dog and into the house?'

'I was in the garden with Liv after supper, and the dog was so used to our visits that he did nothing but wag his tail,' he said. 'When she went back to the house, I waited at the kitchen door and her maid let me in.'

'The maid,' she said with a nod.

'She was quite infatuated with me. And I may have made promises that I had no intention of keeping.'

'But that does not explain why the Duke had to die,' she said. 'What did he ever do to you?'

'Do not waste energy feeling sorry for the man,' Clement replied with a smirk. 'Even his son knew that the world was better off without the old miser. As to my reasons for getting rid of him, I asked for Olivia's hand and he refused me. So, I entered the house as the family was getting ready for bed and paid a visit to his study.' He made a stabbing motion and shrugged. 'I thought, perhaps, his son would be more receptive to my suit. Unfortunately, he wasn't.'

'And what of the maid?' Rachel asked in a choked whisper.

'She assumed that we were to have a liaison. The silly creature even stole one of Olivia's dresses to impress me. She followed me to the study and discovered the truth. She screamed and nearly brought the house down on us. It took some quick thinking on my part to hide the two of us long enough so I could escape in the confusion.'

'This was all about marrying Olivia?' she said, surprised. 'It is a wonder you did not kill Hugh as well. After all, he refused you, just as his father did.'

'It was better to leave him alive and under a cloud of accusation for the crimes I committed. He looked guilty enough when Richard Sterling was found in the river.'

'You did that as well?' She was not really surprised.

'Olivia showed signs of favouring him over me,' he said. 'I could not have that.'

'And why did you kill the maid?'

'She knew too much.' He gave a shrug. 'She witnessed the crime and thought that it entitled her to my full attention. She expected me to run off with her the next day. She thought to blackmail me into it.' He laughed. 'Did she not understand what I was capable of, even after she witnessed it?'

'So, you killed her,' Rachel said, struggling to contain her horror.

'With the ribbon she stole from Olivia's troublesome little sister.' He shook his head. 'Until the last moment, she imagined that we would be together. She should have known that she was never my goal.'

'You love Olivia,' Rachel said.

He gave her a dubious look. 'As much as I can love anyone. At one time, I wanted her luscious body. But, now it has been despoiled by that wretch Solomon, I want my revenge. Thus far, he has proved surprisingly hard to kill. But one day he will be careless and I will end him.'

'You cannot go about exterminating everyone who gets in your way,' she said, amazed.

'So far, it has been a surprisingly successful strategy,' he said. 'And when Scofield's wife is discovered dead it will only confirm what everyone knows: that he is a man that murders any who get too close to him. Perhaps, this time, he will be brought to justice.'

'You will not use my death to discredit Hugh,'

she said, still unsure what it was she could do to prevent it.

Mr Clement smiled, as if picturing the dark future that awaited them. 'I fail to see how you will stop me. As the bodies mount, Scofield's reputation will no longer protect him. Even the House of Lords cannot ignore his crimes. With him hanged, there will be no one for Olivia to turn to except me.'

The idea was mad, of course. If Olivia loved her husband as deeply as Rachel did Hugh, there was no way that widowhood could make her forget him and turn to another for comfort. But it would be a mistake to taunt a madman, so she held her tongue.

He looked at her and sighed. 'But we have talked too long, Your Grace. I think it is time that you tell me where the carriage was headed. And then we must say goodbye.'

'With what you have planned for me, there is very little incentive to help you,' she said, trying to be brave.

'I know from experience that death can be quick and painless, or slow and painful.' He gave her another mad smile. 'I would advise you not to aggravate me.'

'Then I would ask one thing of you first.'

'I suppose a last request is not out of the question.'

'Do not let me die in here. I have just replaced the rug and it would be a shame to ruin it.'

He laughed then, the sincere sound of mirth at odds with what he was contemplating for her. 'How can I refuse the wishes of a lady in her own home? Very well, Your Grace. In what room do you wish to finish this?'

She thought for a moment, trying to decide. 'The green salon, I think.'

'Very well,' he agreed, gesturing with the gun in his hand. 'Lead the way.'

She walked slowly through the door and down the hall towards the salon, listening for the sound of anyone that might save her. But there was nothing but the sound of their footsteps echoing on the marble tile of the hallway. When they arrived at the salon, she hurried into the room ahead of him, slamming the door in his face.

The act bought her only a moment, but she used it to the best of her abilities. By the time he opened the door, she'd grabbed a vase from a nearby side table and threw it at him.

The blow was enough to startle him and he dropped the gun, which discharged as it hit the rug, sending a ball into the plaster beside the fireplace.

He lunged for her then, clawed hands reaching for her throat.

She backed away and her hand flailed behind her, grabbing a poker from the fireplace and bringing it down hard on his head.

He staggered back, more shocked than hurt, then advanced again.

She screamed, praying that someone would hear

her. Then she swung again, harder this time. And then again, as he fell to the floor.

And then, she rushed across the room to the bell-pull, tugged it and collapsed.

Hugh followed the carriage, riding at Solomon's side in silence, his mind focused on the woman he'd left behind.

He should not have left Rachel alone, if only because he knew how much trouble she could get into when he was not watching. She had promised to stay in the house and do nothing other than wait for his return. How could she manage to circumvent an instruction as simple as that?

'Turn back.'

Solomon's voice dragged him from his reverie.

'We are far enough along to manage the trip by ourselves. Let me protect my wife and you can protect your own.' The other man was looking at him with a wry smile.

'If you are sure...' Hugh said, glancing at the road behind him.

'When you have been married as long as I have,' Solomon said, 'You will learn that it is impossible to keep control of everything around you.'

'You have been married barely a month,' Hugh said, smiling.

'And I learn something every day,' Solomon replied. 'Now, go back to London and see to your wife.'

'I will send you word when the Runners have arrested Clement and it is safe to return.'

'Fair enough,' Solomon said, and spurred his horse to catch up with the carriage.

Meanwhile, Hugh turned his horse towards London.

It was almost evening when he arrived at the townhouse. He dismounted and handed his reins to the groom that had accompanied him, then entered through the front door, calling for Rachel.

There was a feeble answering cry from the salon.

He hurried to the door and found her at the windows trying to pull down the drapery cord, an unconscious Clement on the floor at her feet.

'Rachel!'

She looked up at him, her blue eyes wide with panic. She rushed to him then, throwing herself into his arms.

He caught her and held her as she trembled against him.

'I swear, this time I did not do anything. I stayed in the house just like you told me to.' She was muttering apologies into his coat, her arms linked around his waist, swaying against him as if she could barely stand.

'Did he hurt you?' Hugh asked in as calm a tone as he could manage.

She shook her head. 'He wanted to, but I hit him with a poker.'

The man at their feet was moaning, as if consciousness was returning, so Hugh set his wife gently aside. 'Run to the mews and see if you can find a groomsman or two to help me settle this fellow. And send someone to find Pilkington. I am sure he will be interested in your story.'

Then he picked up the pistol that lay on the floor near Clement and grabbed the poker in his other hand for good measure. As Clement sat up, Hugh gave the man a sharp poke in the ribs, sending him skittering towards the nearest wall. 'If you know what is good for you, you will stay down, Clement.'

'Or what?' Clement laughed. 'You will kill me?'

'Perhaps that is what you hope to hear,' Hugh said in a calm, cold voice. 'But then, you would not live to stand trial for the murders you have committed. Do not think you can goad me to fatal violence when justice is close at hand. I am not the man people believe me to be. You, of all people, should know that. But the Runners will not care if you are whole or damaged when they take you away, and if you give me reason to act you will live to regret it.'

Rachel returned then with two grooms and a stout rope. The Runners arrived a short time later, and Hugh sat beside Rachel, holding her hand as she related the gruesome story that Clement had revealed to her. The inspector listened in silence, then signalled that the suspect be manacled and escorted from the room.

Before he left, he turned to Hugh, head bowed in

respect. 'I apologise for my misunderstanding of the situation, Your Grace.'

Hugh resisted the urge to laugh in response and tell him that a few words could not make up for the trials of the last two years. But then he turned and looked at Rachel, who was looking at him with the same devotion as always, and Pilkington's former opinion of him did not seem so very important. So, he dismissed the man with a smile and a nod.

Then, he was alone with his wife.

Rachel stared at Hugh as the door closed, eager to see what his reaction would be now that he was finally free of the rumours that had circulated about him for so long.

But, before she could ask, he had pulled her from her seat on the divan and wrapped her in his arms for a passionate kiss. 'I should never have left you alone.' He paused just long enough to murmur the words against her throat. 'When I think that I might have lost you...'

'It is all right,' Rachel murmured, trying not to tremble. 'I was not hurt.'

'But you could have been,' he said, running his hands lightly over her body as if to reassure himself that she was real and whole. 'If anything had happened to you because I was too foolish to find the truth of this...'

'Do not say that word,' she replied, placing a finger on his lips. 'You are nobody's fool.'

'And you, as always, are too good to me,' he said, kissing her hand. 'We could have been together all this time.'

'Is that what you truly wanted?' Rachel asked hopefully.

'More than life,' he replied, slowly backing her towards the divan.

'On our wedding night—'

'I lied,' he interrupted before she could finish. 'I wanted to hurt you so it would be easier to push you away. As I said before, I was a fool.' He turned then and sat, drawing her into his lap. 'But a fool in love,' he added, adjusting her so that she was sprawled on top of him.

'You love me,' she whispered, relieved.

'And you love me,' he said softly. 'You have been telling me so with every fibre of your being, even when I deserved it least, and defended me when I would not defend myself.'

He was tugging at the hem of her dress now, pulling it up over her knees, so she tugged it down again. 'We mustn't,' she said, surprised to see a roguish glint in his eyes that had not been there for years. 'Not here, at least,' she amended.

'The servants are gone and we are finally alone,' he reminded her. 'We can do whatever we want, wherever we want.'

'How utterly shameless,' she said, but she could not help smiling.

'We have nothing to be ashamed of. We are married, after all. And if you sit thusly, there will be no question of discomfort, as there was the last time.' He leaned back in his seat and adjusted her so she straddled his hips. 'You will be in complete control of what happens.'

She wondered if she should explain that the last time had not been painful in the physical sense. And then, she realised what he had just said. 'You would relinquish control?' she whispered, amazed.

'I have learned that letting you do what you want can be pleasurable for both of us,' he said, kissing his way along her jawline.

'And is this true of other women?' she asked, her breath quickening as he undid the buttons on the back of her gown.

'You are worrying about Martine again.' He growled against her skin. 'Other than that brief visit in Vauxhall, I have not seen her in over a year.' His hand came down to cup her bottom, pressing her hips to his. 'And if you are very good, or perhaps very naughty, I will do things with you that I never considered with her.'

The suggestion sent a thrill through Rachel and she reached between her legs to the buttons of his breeches.

He gave a grunt of approval and pushed her dress off her shoulders, running his hands over the bare skin he'd exposed. The room was chilly, but her body was hot from his touch and she wanted to shed every last stitch of clothing, to be near him as she had been in bed.

But that would take too long. His gentle kisses had reached her breasts and a rush of heat passed through her, settling between her legs. She bundled her skirts out of the way and settled over him, reaching between them to touch his manhood and guide it into her body, which was wet and ready.

He entered her with a long, slow thrust and they were one again, as she had always hoped they would be. He stilled then, waiting. Waiting for her.

At first she revelled in the sensation, afraid that movement might spoil what they already had. Then she realised that by flexing her thighs she could control the thrusts, just as he had promised. So she braced her hands on his shoulders and moved, writhing against him as he palmed her breasts, urging her on.

The tension was growing between them, and Rachel could not resist the opportunity to reach between them and touch herself, driving her body to grip his, drawing him in as she moved around him. She could feel him nearing a climax as well. His breathing quickened and his body shook with trying to prolong the inevitable.

Then, when she was teetering on the brink and feared he would push her away, he drew her closer, coming into her in a rush of heat that tipped her over the edge too.

It was as wonderful as she'd always known it

would be. She kissed him then, free of the fears that had haunted her since they'd married.

He did not bother to withdraw but laid his head on her breast and sighed happily. 'Rachel,' he said, and there was none of the usual frustration in his tone.

'Hugh,' she replied, tugging on his cravat.

'I should write to Solomon and tell him they are safe.'

She sighed and climbed off his lap, taking his hand and pulling him towards the writing desk. 'You have time for a short note before bed time.'

He smiled in surprise, swept her off her feet and into his arms. 'Or I can write to him tomorrow.' Then he carried her towards the stairs and her room.

Epilogue

'Rachel.' They had been married for months, and still Hugh could not manage his wife. At the moment, she was balancing on a ladder, hanging a kissing bow in the doorway of the Scofield Manor library, paying no heed to the risks she was taking.

'The guests will be here tomorrow,' Rachel reminded him. 'And I cannot trust the footman to hang this straight.'

Since it was pointless to argue with her, he went to steady the ladder. 'Think of the baby,' he warned, laying a protective hand on her stomach.

'The baby and I will be fine,' she assured him, giving the satin ribbons a final tug. 'We are not made of glass.'

She was probably right. But the fact that he was to be a father was still a novelty to him, and he could not help feeling protective. 'Next time you wish to hang decorations, come to me for help.'

She smiled and stepped down to the floor again. 'I

just want everything to be perfect for the house party. It is Christmas, after all, and I want it to be special.'

'I am sure that it will be fine,' he assured her. 'Some of the people are only coming to gawk at us.'

'They have no reason to,' she reminded him. 'Since the arrest of Mr Clement, I have never met so many apologetic acquaintances eager to get on our good side.'

He smiled. 'I doubt that it will make a difference to some people. They have believed the worst for too long. But it is easier for me to manage now that I know the truth.'

'You will see the change by next season,' she said with a smile. 'When we throw a ball, people will be clamouring for invitations.'

'Rachel,' he said in a tone of mock warning. 'Who gave you permission to hold a ball?'

'You will, I am sure, if I ask when we are in bed tonight,' she answered with a grin.

He grabbed her then and kissed her, for she was right. In or out of bed, he could deny her nothing.

The sound of the first guests arriving came from the hall. Rachel grabbed his hand and tugged Hugh into the hall to greet his sisters and their husbands and the newest addition to the family—his niece, Emily Castell.

He stared in amazement at the infant squalling in Peg's arms, still finding it hard to believe that his youngest sister was now a mother. As far as he knew, Olivia had not been similarly blessed. But then, she and Solomon had been married only a few weeks longer than Rachel and him. It was early, yet.

Rachel hugged each of the girls in turn, cooed at the baby and smiled at her brothers-in-law. She was a warm and genuine hostess and he could not help but be proud of how easily she managed.

For Hugh, it was somewhat more difficult. Castell and Solomon looked at him with polite curiosity and each offered a greeting. 'Scofield.'

He smiled back at them, reaching out to shake their hands. 'Gentlemen, welcome to my home.'

At this, Solomon could not help but laugh. 'I am sorry, Your Grace, but I never thought I would hear those words from you.'

'Then I doubt you will expect these words either,' Hugh replied, pausing to gather his nerve. 'Please call me Hugh, as your wives do. We are family now, after all.'

His guests fell silent as they tried to digest his offer, and then the room broke into laughter along with Solomon.

'Is my hospitality so strange as that?' Hugh asked, confused.

'As strange as if my dog began to talk,' Olivia said, showing him no mercy.

'You are the dangerous Duke of Scofield, after all,' Peg added with a stern expression. 'The unsmiling terror of London.' Then she handed him the baby, who burbled happily in his uneasy grip.

While holding a child, he did not feel the least bit

dangerous. He felt terrified at what was to come. But it was a happy sort of terror, if such a thing could be, full of possibilities as well as risks. He beamed down at the child and said, 'You may call me Uncle Hugh, when you are able.'

'As I have been telling everyone who will listen, Hugh is not the least bit dangerous,' Rachel said as he passed the child back to her mother.

'I cannot afford to be dangerous.' Hugh smiled at his family. 'My wife will not allow it. And you must know, gentlemen, that there is no point in arguing with a woman who loves you once she decides to change your life. And now, let us all go in by the fire and enjoy what I am sure will be the best Christmas ever.'

* * * * *

If you enjoyed this story, be sure to read the other books in Christine Merrill's Secrets of the Duke's Family miniseries

Lady Margaret's Mysterious Gentleman
Lady Olivia's Forbidden Protector

And why not check out her other great reads?

Vows to Save Her Reputation
"Their Mistletoe Reunion" *in* Snowbound Surrender
The Brooding Duke of Danforth